MASKS AND MIRRORS

KATE MOSEMAN

FORTUNELLA PRESS

Previously published as *Undercover Royal*.

Cover by ArcaneCovers.com

ISBN 978-1-957320-12-0 (ebook)

ISBN 978-1-957320-23-6 (paperback)

Fortunella Press

For Ivy, my fire mouse

1

If you have to wake up to someone staring at you while you sleep, they should at least be good-looking. It takes the edge off the urge to scream.

It does not, however, make up for drool on your pillow, holes in your sleep shirt, and rats' nests in your hair. Especially when the intruder is dressed in what looks like rough silk, and he's wearing a gold crown.

A *prince*. Why did he have to be a prince?

I yanked the sheet over my head. "Berron, you colossal idiot. What in God's name do you think you're doing in my bedroom at this hour of the morning?"

"Waking you up." His light but rich baritone sparkled with amusement. "I should think that was obvious, my Zelda."

"Not your Zelda. Get out of my room." And where was my dog? Weren't dogs supposed to alert you to intruders? I pulled the sheet down just far enough to peek out.

Jester, my miniature poodle, was happily snuggled in Berron's arms like a little black lamb being carried by a shepherd. He gazed adoringly at Berron.

"Some watchdog you are," I said.

Jester added insult to injury by delicately licking Berron's chin.

"Are you ready to go?"

I shot him a look. "Do I look ready to go?"

He shrugged. "I'm no expert on your state of dress, or undress, as the case may be."

"And—go *where*, by the way?"

"To the Fortress of Apples, of course. Where it all begins."

I nearly asked *Where what begins?*, but I stopped myself. I wouldn't give him the satisfaction. The Gentry seemed to revel in being mysterious. Or at least this one did. "You wake me out of a sound sleep and expect me to go skipping off to another realm on no notice whatsoever? Were you planning to let me put on pants?"

He grinned.

"Don't answer that." I threw back the sheet and sat up, modesty and holey pajamas be damned. "Put the dog down and go wait downstairs like a civilized person."

Berron scratched behind Jester's ears. "But he likes me. And I'm not a civilized person."

"You're a prince, aren't you? So act like it."

"Then I would just order you to come with me now, and have you banished if you disobey."

I squeezed my eyes shut and took a deep breath. "If you are still standing there when I open my eyes, I promise I will kill you."

A whisper of sound. A whiff of fresh air, touched with greenness.

I opened my eyes. Berron was gone. So was Jester.

But the Gentry prince had left a signature. Deep green ivy climbed as high as the old-fashioned crown moulding, as if my bedroom had been drawn into a hidden forest. The heart-shaped leaves, still freshly shimmering with green and gold magic, shivered in an invisible breeze.

Point one to the fae prince for theatrics.

I sighed, threw a pillow across the room, where it bounced harmlessly off the vines and fell to the floor. No use in delaying the inevitable. I got dressed, carefully laced my Doc Martens, and headed for the stairs.

A bright laugh bubbled up the stairwell. Poppy, my roommate, must have run into Berron.

There they were, when I reached the first floor: comfortably seated on the couch, with Poppy's Irish wolfhound, Georgiana, sitting between them, and Jester racing around madly, chasing a ball on the floor. Morning sunbeams shot across the room and dust motes swirled through the light.

Poppy caught sight of me and put her cup on the coffee table. "Oh! Zelda—you'll never guess—I can't read his mind! Isn't it marvelous?"

Berron lifted his crown like a normal man would tip his hat.

I rubbed my eyes to remove the last of the sleep. "Are all the Gentry like that?"

"As far as I know," he said.

"How lovely," sighed Poppy. "A real vacation from other people's thoughts."

"You should come," said Berron, his face lighting up.

"Come where?" said Poppy.

"With us." He gestured to me.

"Oh, I *should*." Poppy turned to me with naked hope in her eyes.

This was spiraling out of control. Next thing you knew, the dogs would be coming along.

"And we'll bring the dogs!" Poppy exclaimed.

"Poppy, stop reading my mind."

"You got too close. I couldn't help it," she added, primly.

I took a few careful steps backward, out of range. A long squeak sounded as I stepped on Jester's ball. Jester dove for it and I lifted my foot just in time. "I mean, Poppy coming would be great, but the shop's just getting on its feet, and I only have James helping me out..."

"Who's James?" Berron asked.

"Reluctant member of the Blessed," said Poppy.

"Do you want me to stake him for you?"

"He's a *reluctant* one, not one with a death wish. And he fought off Prospero and friends while you and I had our little chat by the Mirror," I said.

"I shall not stake him, then." He leaned over and peered into Poppy's cup. "Is this coffee? Can I have some?"

I folded my arms. "Are you placing an order? Does this look like a restaurant?"

He got to his feet, startling Jester, who abandoned his ball and began jumping at Berron like a furry black pogo stick. "No, it's just that—Jester, sit."

Jester immediately sat on his haunches, quivering with the joy of following Berron's instructions. I couldn't help but be impressed. Jester only obeyed my commands when he felt like it, or when I had a treat in my hand.

"There's no coffee where we are going," Berron finished. "So I thought I'd drink as much as I could while I'm here."

"No *coffee*?" said Poppy.

"Couldn't you bring it in?" I asked.

Berron made a face. "I need espresso. We don't have machines."

I rolled my eyes. "Come on, Your Princeliness. It's in the kitchen."

When Berron followed, Jester trotted at his heels. The three of us entered the kitchen, passing by the little sign Poppy had bought that said *Eat Dessert First*. I cornered Berron by the coffee machine. "Listen," I said, quietly so Poppy couldn't overhear. "The last time I got a friend involved in something, bad things happened. I can't let Poppy go galloping off into some unknown danger."

"But she wants to go—"

"Remember Daniel?"

"Bah." Berron waved his hand. "Daniel is a fool."

"It doesn't matter whether he's a fool or not, he's *my* friend, and it's *my* fault that he became collateral damage."

Berron smirked. "You didn't deny he was a fool."

I rubbed my forehead in an attempt to ward off an oncoming headache. "This is all beside the point."

"Which is?"

"The point is—I'm not putting anyone else in harm's way. And you have to respect that, or I'm not coming."

He tweaked a piece of my hair. "Yes, Zelda."

"I mean it."

He kissed my forehead and pivoted to the coffee machine.

"And don't kiss me."

"I am a creature of nature. I cannot help it. Besides, you kissed me first."

"I didn't *kiss* you, I uncovered your deception. Kissing just happened to be the medium."

Berron hummed to himself as he worked the machine. The tune was familiar.

"I can see you're not listening."

Then the hum turned into a song, and I recognized the lyrics immediately: *Oh how lovely is the evening, is the evening, when the bells are sweetly ringing, sweetly ringing...*

Goosebumps crawled over my skin. My grandmother's lullaby. "Why are you singing that?"

"Hm?"

I poked him in his broad back. "Why are you singing that?"

"Why do we sing anything? And also, *ow*." The coffee machine burbled and the good-morning scent filled the air as he poured.

"Give me that," I said.

"I was going to," he replied calmly, turning around. "I can see how much you need it."

"Shut up. I have to go see Daniel this morning." I reached for the cup he held out, but he pulled it back.

"Why do you have to see *Daniel*?"

"Because when you turn someone into a"—I leaned forward and whispered—"a vampire..." My voice returned to normal. "You're responsible for them."

"He's a grown man."

"So are you. And yet here you are, cadging my coffee, telling me I need to go save the world."

"Please give Daniel my best." By the mischievous look in his eyes, Berron's best meant *tie his shoelaces together and push him in the deepest lake in Central Park*.

"I will," I said, rebelliously.

"You do that."

Our gazes tangled for an uncomfortable few seconds. I didn't need to touch him to feel the echo of green and gold ecstasy I'd felt that day in the back room of West Side Sandwiches. All the more reason to turn away. "Drink your coffee. Come back tomorrow."

"My lady dismisses me! I am cut to the quick." He mimed stabbing himself in the chest, and staggered back against the kitchen counter.

I laughed despite myself. Maybe I couldn't trust him, but a rock would have had trouble resisting his charm. "Get out, Gentry."

"I go, I go." He made over-the-top bows as he backed out of the kitchen.

Jester, who had been sniffing around the base of the cabinets in search of crumbs, trotted over and looked up at me. His fluffy ears lifted, and he cocked his head as if asking a question.

I scooped him up in his preferred carrying position—his hip balanced on mine, my arm threaded under his body and one hand supporting his chest. Jester was half a baby, half a puppy, and as relaxed as a sack of flour. He turned his head and sniffed behind my ear, which tickled.

"What do you think I should do, boy?"

Jester really only had two approaches: bite it or kiss it. Sometimes both.

We had more in common than I liked to admit.

2

It's not always the things you expect that bring back the strongest memories. Walking to Daniel's didn't do it. The thick haze outside was the same as it had been since I arrived in New York. Seeing the doorman didn't trigger anything either, nor did riding the elevator up and up and up.

No, it was the hallway on Daniel's floor, when the elevator doors slid closed behind me. The hallway, with its closed-in air and plush but forgettable carpeting. An in-between place, neither here nor there. You can't stay in a place like that indefinitely. You have to choose: go forward, or return to somewhere else entirely.

Sometimes the doors close behind you and there's no going back.

The hotel-like air seemed to hold me in its grasp. I couldn't even reach out to knock—but I didn't have to. Daniel's door clicked open.

No one should be wearing a three-piece suit on a weekend morning unless they're going to a wedding. Especially with a red silk handkerchief folded into sharp points and precisely tucked into the breast pocket. Daniel had always been a sharp dresser, but why, oh, why did vampires have to be so *extra*? I felt under-dressed in denim cutoffs and a black tank.

I lifted a soft-sided lunch box I'd carried all the way from Poppy's. "I brought brunch."

Daniel's nostrils flared ever so slightly. "I know. Come in."

I crossed the threshold and carefully set the lunch box on the bar. "I found a source. Poppy knew someone selling it under the table from a lab."

"Excellent," said Daniel. He unzipped the lunch box, and his gaze darted avidly over the contents.

"Do you want to go eat first, and then—" I stopped, because he was already pulling out and uncorking the first vial.

He threw back the blood like a shot of tequila.

"Or you can just have it right now, that's fine too," I finished.

"Does this bother you?" Daniel lowered the vial and paused.

"No, no. Not at all." I smiled to cover the slight queasiness that rolled through my belly.

He set the first vial aside and picked up the next. "Yes, it does." He uncapped it without breaking eye contact. Then he tilted his head back and drained it. The second vial rattled to the bar, empty. "Would you rather me get it some other way?" A bitter smile. "Do you volunteer?"

"We're not that desperate." The vision of what that might look like sent my stomach into further flip-flops. I slammed the lid on those thoughts and concentrated on keeping a neutral expression.

He chuckled and opened a third vial. "I'm only kidding."

It was an effort not to exhale loudly. Daniel's conversion hadn't made him a stranger, but I was still feeling my way around his new edges. I moved to one of the floor-to-ceiling windows so he didn't think I was staring at him while he "ate."

Midtown unfolded below, blue sky gleaming on reflective buildings. Beautiful view. Untouchable through the thick windows. I laid my hand on the glass and felt the chill from the air conditioning compete with the heat outside.

"Leaving fingerprints?"

"Something to remember me by." I turned as Daniel approached. All traces of blood were gone. Even the vials had been packed away. I could pretend everything was the same.

Until I met his gaze again, and it was still red.

"I may be going out of town for a while," I said.

"Oh?"

"Victorine will make sure you have what you need—"

Daniel looked away.

"Is something wrong?"

"I don't need Lady Victorine to babysit me."

I scoffed. "Who else would bring you—uh—*takeout*?"

"Squeamish, Zelda?" He moved a fraction closer. "Just call it what it is. We're alone. No one can hear you."

It wasn't a threat. It wasn't. But that didn't stop the hairs from standing up on my neck. "Fine, *blood*. Happy?"

"Where are you going?"

"Who are you, my mother?"

"You're doing something interesting. You've got that look." He studied my face, then frowned. "It's that guy, isn't it? The one from the restaurant. Berron."

"So?"

"You know I'm interested in all things magical." He sat on the couch, his arms spread comfortably on the backs of the cushions, and regarded me with his red-tinged gaze. "So tell me about it."

I hesitated. This magic world, though familiar from childhood, was still new to me. I was still learning the rules. Still learning who to trust. The Blessed and the Gentry were enemies—could I discuss Berron with Daniel? Or Victorine? Or even James, who wanted out, like the Blessed were the mob?

Yet I'd known Daniel before all that. We were friends, ex-lovers, and friends once again. It had to count for *something*. The fact that he was a vampire now couldn't erase history.

"Berron says there's something very wrong with where the Gentry live. He wants me to come with him and try to fix it."

Daniel's eyebrows shot up. "He wants *you* to fix it? Why?"

"Something to do with the Mirror. My grandmother's magic."

"How?"

I shrugged.

"Do you trust him?"

"*Trust* him?"

"Trust him enough to go with him, alone, into a place you've never been before—where no human has been in a generation, at least—and dangers you know absolutely nothing about?"

"Of course I trust him."

The strength of Daniel's skeptical look would have peeled the paint off a car.

"Okay," I admitted. "I *kind of* trust him."

Daniel shook his head. "You shouldn't go alone."

I flung my hand up. "Look what happens when I bring other people into things!"

He was off the couch and closing in before I could back away. "Exactly. All the more reason for you not to be alone."

"I'm not bringing Poppy."

"I'm not suggesting Poppy." He was so close I could smell his exquisite cologne.

"Oh, no. Don't even think about it."

"It makes sense." Why did his voice sound like a tiger purr?

"Stop it."

"Stop what?"

I placed one hand on his chest and, with steady pressure, gave myself some personal distance. "That. All that. Also, I don't need your protection."

He smirked. "I'm not your protection. I'm your sacrificial lamb. If you run into a dragon, it can eat me instead."

"Forget dragons. I'm tempted to give you and Berron sticks and let you beat each other to death. Maybe then you can be friends. Don't laugh." I gave him a severe look as he ignored the command completely.

"I do like Berron," he said. "The man knows his way around a piece of wood. I just don't *trust* Berron."

"That sounds like damning with faint praise and you know it."

"I call it like I see it. Do you need to ask his permission for me to come?"

I almost took the bait, then checked myself. "You know I don't. You're just trying to rile me up."

"Are you riled, Zelda?"

"No."

I was. I was very riled.

Or something.

He approached with open hands, carefully, as if I were a cornered cat. "This is your world. I'm just living in it. But I *can* be helpful to you." When I didn't push him away, he took my hands in his. Red thorny vines of vampire magic spiraled from his hands and wrapped around mine, burning like dipping your hands into a too-hot bath. But as it traveled through my whole being, the too-hot sensation melted into being just right.

I bit my lip to stop the sigh of contentment that threatened to escape. I should have pulled away. Instead, I held on, letting the magic of the Blessed do its rejuvenating work. It felt *so* good. My eyes drifted closed, and I swayed on my feet.

"See?" he said, gently.

"Mm." Somehow I'd ended up leaning against him. A more sober Zelda, somewhere deep in the cooler part of my brain, told me I was probably making some kind of mistake. Sober Zelda wanted to know why James and Victorine didn't make me feel like this when they shared their magic.

Sober Zelda could sit down and be quiet for a while.

"I can do this whenever you need me to."

"Helpful," I murmured, the word coming out fuzzy. With an effort, I pulled my hands free, then stepped back and cleared my throat, businesslike. "Very helpful. Doesn't mean you're coming with me."

"You know where to find me."

"That I do. But now I have to go to the shop. You're not my only responsibility." I raked my hair away from my face and wished the vampire magic would settle down instead of dancing in my veins like champagne. Distracting.

Hunger came to the rescue. There's nothing like a good tummy growl to focus the mind. I hadn't had anything but coffee yet, and since the breakfast rush was mostly over, I could get behind the counter and make whatever I wanted: Denver omelet bagel sandwich, breakfast pigs-in-a-blanket made with buttermilk pancakes and sausages, handheld eggs Benedict dripping with Hollandaise sauce.

"Are you all right?" asked Daniel.

I blinked.

"Your eyes went out of focus."

"Thinking deep thoughts." I scooped up the soft-sided cooler, now quite a bit lighter. "I'll be back with more blood." This time, I barely hesitated over the word.

"Don't do anything I wouldn't do."

"Is that a limitation or a permission slip?"

"Lady's choice."

"Don't you know, Daniel?" I paused, cocked my head. "Everything is lady's choice." I patted his cheek and left him there in his glass tower.

I had to return to earth to see to my own hunger.

3

I held open the door as customers trooped out with paper to-go bags and steaming coffees. When the line dispersed, I entered West Side Sandwiches. The bells rattled as the door swung closed behind me.

Every chair, every table, every fork and spork was part of my domain, and I felt them all like extensions of myself. Hard-fought and restored. My grandma's restaurant, now mine.

"Hello!" Lily called from her station at the register. She worked the counter to earn extra money, and with her cheerful demeanor and always-on energy, she was a natural.

I went behind the counter and gave her a quick hug around the shoulders. "Morning, kiddo." I stepped away and ran my fingers around the frame of the original occupational license, the one Grandma had changed to say *West Side 'Wiches* instead of *West Side Sandwiches*. "Another day, another sandwich, Grandma," I murmured with satisfaction.

I was home.

"Hey, boss," said James, flourishing the large turner. He looked as natural as if he'd been born in chef whites, and he seemed utterly content to scramble eggs and fry hash browns at all hours of the day and night.

I hung up my coat and took an apron off the hook. "What'd I miss?"

"You had a visitor," said James, with a meaningful look.

"Oh?" I pulled the apron strings around.

"She went for a walk," Lily said. "Said she would come back later. Your friend? From the grand opening?"

My fingers froze mid-knot. "What friend?"

"This one," said a smooth and cultured voice. Late morning sunlight backlit Victorine and turned her into a shadow. She shifted, and the change in angle revealed large sunglasses, an elegantly knotted silk scarf, a luxurious camel overcoat over tailored slacks, and what were no doubt very expensive shoes.

Lily watched with round-eyed curiosity as Victorine came closer.

"Where were you?" Victorine asked.

I washed my hands, taking my time, refusing to hurry. "Daniel's," I said, drying my hands. I reached for two eggs.

"And?"

"He was fine." I cracked the first egg too hard, and the inside exploded. Cold liquid egg dripped from my hand.

James slid up beside me and took the bowl, the unbroken egg, and the broken eggshell. "I'll make it," he said. He knew what I liked.

I washed the egg off my hand, then steered Victorine to a corner table. "You can't always just drop in. My cousin's daughter helps out from time to time. She can't know about any of this."

"I'm surprised it doesn't run in the family."

"Even if it does—"

"I'm only teasing. Calm yourself." She removed her sunglasses and set them on the table. When she met my gaze, her eyes glinted red. "How is Daniel?"

I shrugged. "How is anyone after being converted?" She waited for me to say more. "What do you want from me? He's fine."

Her lips pressed together. She paused, as if about to say something, then checked herself and appeared to switch tactics. "And you?"

"What about me?"

"Don't play coy. You're not good at it."

"Fine." I leaned closer and lowered my voice. "I'm going to need access to the Mirror."

Her eyebrows arched. "Already?"

"Prince Charming wants me to go with him and have a look around."

"Why now?"

"I assume it's because his realm is dying and he'd prefer that it didn't."

Victorine gave a faint smile. "All realms are dying. It's only a matter of time."

"Great. I'll be sure to tell him that."

"Who will go with you?"

"You're the second person to ask me that."

"Daniel?"

"Right."

She tapped her chin thoughtfully with a manicured fingernail. "Did he volunteer to go?"

"Yes." I paused. "Why do you ask?"

Her cool gaze held mine without blinking. "How well do you know him?"

"Better than almost anyone. We go way back..." I trailed off, watching the calculation in her eyes. "What are you getting at?"

Time stretched until I thought sunbeams might move across the floor by the time Victorine answered. "What has happened to Daniel—it *changes* people."

"No kidding."

"Listen to me." Her stillness was almost hypnotic. "The transition—the conversion—is not just what you see on the surface. Beliefs change. Priorities change. A person you thought you knew becomes a stranger. It can be startling."

I didn't like startling.

"All I'm saying," Victorine continued, "is that Daniel's sudden interest in accompanying you is curious."

"He's always been interested in—that sort of thing," I said, rather than use the word *magic*.

"Perhaps he has. But think about it in another way: He can no longer leave the island of Manhattan. He is trapped. Do you not think that chafes him? He is a man of the world. Will he be content with such a limitation?"

"So what if he isn't? He's stuck with it."

"Not if he aligns with Lord Prospero."

At that moment, James dropped off a plate of two eggs, sunny side up, on a toasted everything bagel with a slice of cold-smoked salmon, a schmear of cream cheese, and a sprinkling of fresh dill.

And my mouth had gone so dry I couldn't eat a damn bite of it. "Not after what they did to him," I said. I remembered holding him, in that stuffy Gramercy Park apartment, while his life faded. I shuddered, shook it off. "He would never do that."

"Do you know that, or are you convincing yourself?"

"I know," I shot back.

"Then where is your appetite?"

I scooped up the decadent sandwich, fixed her with a glare, and bit off as big a bite as I could chew. The runny yolks burst and dripped down the bread.

"And you say my kind are messy eaters," said Victorine.

I chewed and swallowed, wishing James had thought to bring some orange juice over. And Advil, for my developing headache. "Hilarious."

"I think you should bring him with you."

"What?" I laughed. "He is not going with me."

"You could keep an eye on him."

"I don't *want* to keep an eye on him. I have enough to do." I gestured with the drippy sandwich. "Why don't *you* keep an eye on him?"

"Because he trusts you. Because you know him."

"You want me to take him on a—a *field trip*? At this rate I'll be bringing half the population of New York."

"He could use a distraction."

"A minder, you mean."

"It will keep him out of trouble."

I made a disbelieving noise. "And what if Berron doesn't think this is such a great idea?"

"Convince him."

"Not my strong point," I said. "Sarcasm, bossiness, the occasional physical altercation, yes. Convincing, no."

"You convinced Daniel to let you stay with him in the first place."

Oh, she was good. Steel-trap logic and nuclear-grade guilt.

James approached the table. "Lady Victorine," he murmured, addressing her first, with a ghost of a bow, before turning to me. "Is everything all right? Do you need anything?"

"Victorine thinks I should take Daniel through the Mirror."

James' eyes widened, and he cast a glance over his shoulder at Lily. "You can't talk like that where people can hear—"

"It's all right, James," Victorine said. "Zelda likes to live on the edge."

I pointed the remaining half-circle of the bagel sandwich at her. "Any more sarcasm from you, madam, and I'll eighty-six you."

"Zelda?" Lily called from across the room. The morning rush had subsided completely, and we were the only people left in the restaurant.

"Yeah?"

"I think... something's on fire?"

As the words hit my brain, a thin, acrid scent of smoke curled into my nose. "Oh, my God!" I pushed back my chair and ran, James hard on my heels.

The typical kitchen fire starts in a pan. I'd seen that kind before—flames can shoot three feet high in seconds, triggering the overhead fire suppression system. But this wasn't that. Instead, a thin sheet of fire covered the griddle like a burning blanket.

Weirdly, the blanket appeared to have moving lumps under it, as if there were balls rolling underneath.

"I swear I didn't leave anything on there," said James.

"Get the baking sheets." I quickly turned off the griddle and slammed the nearest pot lids onto the fire. Though they snuffed the fire in small circles, they weren't big enough to put the whole thing out. A fire extinguisher was the last resort; it would create an awful mess that would take at least a day to clean up. But if I had to, I had to.

"Here." James held out a baking sheet.

I used tongs to move the pot lids, then took the baking sheet and slid it onto the left side of the griddle.

The fire didn't just get snuffed. It appeared to *flee* to the right side of the griddle.

With a series of high-pitched squeaky noises.

I held my hand out for another baking sheet. "Did you hear that?"

"Hear what?" said James, handing me the metal tray.

"Nothing." I slowly slid the second one onto the griddle, and watched the fire tumble over itself to get away from the oncoming tray.

Fire didn't normally do that.

It also didn't have... a *tail*? And... *ears*? And a body like a ping-pong ball toddling around on tiny kangaroo legs?

"Take Lily and Victorine outside. For safety. Don't let anyone in."

"Don't you want me to stay and help?"

"I got this." They left as the fire continued to crackle and squeak. When they were gone, I corralled the fire into an even smaller space.

Then I carefully, oh, so carefully, scooped up the fire in the palm of my hand. Thanks to Poppy's fire magic, the heat felt no worse than an insulated cup of hot coffee.

The flames wavered and re-formed.

Tiny kangaroo legs. Ping-pong ball body. Head the size of a large marble. Ears like perfect periwinkle shells. Itty-bitty forepaws. And a trailing, miniature tail of flames.

A *fire mouse*?

I'd never heard of such a thing.

It cocked its little head and made grooming motions with its front paws. Flickers of fire, like ignited match heads, popped where its paws passed. It turned a circle in my palm and made curious peeping noises.

Since scooping up the little guy—gal?—the fire on the griddle had died down. I held the mouse with one hand, and with the other, I slid the baking sheet over the remaining flames on the griddle. They went out without a fuss.

But what to do with a magical fire mouse? Too cute to snuff—but if I let it go, it could run into the walls and burn down the whole block. I had to do *something*. James and company would be poking their heads back inside, out of sheer curiosity, if not concern for my safety, any minute.

I wasn't a fire witch. But I'd played with borrowed fire magic enough to know that when you held a fire in your hand, then put it out, you could conjure it back up with a thought.

I stroked the mouse's head with a fingertip. "All right, kiddo. Naptime."

Peep.

I cupped my other hand gently over the mouse. Then I closed my eyes. This was no different than when I'd conjured a flame to follow James deep into the abandoned church. This was just letting it go back to where it came from, back to wherever magical fire existed when it wasn't *here*. The heat in my hands dwindled—but in some way it was migrating *through* me, and unlike the plain fire I'd held in the church, this one had personality.

Peep.

I opened my hands. Like a magician's trick, the fire mouse was gone.

Had that last peep been out loud?

Or in my head?

4

The next day, because of the fire mouse incident, Poppy insisted I should be examined by the head honcho of her witches' club. It wouldn't be my first trip to the League of Women's Welfare, also known as the Ladies Who Witch, but it would be the first time I'd be officially introduced.

Tourists crowded the path as we crossed into Central Park. We dodged the photo-takers and continued on our way.

"I don't see why your boss needs to see a fire mouse," I said. "I mean, she must see all kinds of things. It's practically normal to her. Boring, even."

"It *isn't*," Poppy insisted. "I've never heard of anything like it. And she's not my boss. She's—she's my *friend*. I did a favor for her once. Then she let me join the LWW." She did a little twirl on the sidewalk.

"They sure put on one hell of a charity bazaar," I said, remembering the day Jester ate magical good-luck clover.

"Wait until you see the rest of the building. It's marvelous, I tell you. Simply marvelous." Poppy stopped walking to watch a gaggle of small children playing on the grass.

I stopped, too, shading my eyes from the sun. New York took summer seriously, collecting the heat in all the concrete and then radiantly blasting it back. As humid as Florida, but somehow even more stifling.

The little monsters were maybe around seven or eight years old, that last age when they're not quite self-conscious yet. Girls and boys held their hands up like they were holding reins, then galloped across the grassy field, whinnying and snorting all the way.

"Oh, that looks like *fun*," Poppy said. She grabbed hold of my arm. "Come on."

"You're not serious." A second look convinced me that she was. "I don't gallop. Also, it's five hundred degrees out here."

"Don't be scared, Zelda," she said, with the air of an aristocratic nanny. "Playing horsey can't hurt you."

"I'm not scared—hey!" Her grip tightened on my arm, and Poppy launched into the field, dragging me along with her until I had no choice but to match her gallop for gallop to avoid falling on my face.

"Tally-ho!" shouted Poppy.

Suddenly, the momentum kicked in and I was galloping along like Black Beauty, laughing helplessly, as we scattered the kids in all directions. We thundered onward, two grown women with more momentum than they knew what to do with, until Poppy's straw hat blew off and a set of tall boulders blocked our way forward.

Poppy doubled over, breathing hard but triumphant. "See? I told you it was fun."

With the magic of the Blessed still flaming its way through my veins, I was barely winded. "You were right." When Poppy straightened, I gave her a light punch on the shoulder. "You great big galloping idiot."

"Who's big?" she cried, pretending to be offended. "I throw down the gauntlet to you, sir." She looked down at herself, as if to find a gauntlet to throw, then fixed her gaze on my head right before neatly knocking my black West Side Sandwiches ball cap off with her hand. "Aha!"

I lunged at her, and she galloped off, laughing, to retrieve her own hat, which was now tumbling in a welcome morning breeze.

I scooped mine up and replaced it. Of all the things I hadn't expected to happen when I moved to Manhattan, galloping through Central Park with New York's sunniest English fire witch would have been the least expected. The season hadn't even changed yet, but everything else had.

Poppy's voice came from behind me. "I got my hat." She brandished it triumphantly, then tugged it onto her head. "Onward!"

We reached the eastern edge of Central Park and crossed 5th Avenue to enter the Upper East Side.

The wrought iron gates of the League of Women's Welfare were closed and locked, unlike the day when the red carpet had literally been rolled out between the ornate gold-painted iron *L W W* mono-gram.

Poppy pressed the call button on the speaker mounted by the door.

We waited as fancy people with fancier dogs strolled past.

Finally, the speaker squawked. "League of Women's Welfare. May I help you?"

Poppy pushed the button, her manner becoming haughty even before she spoke. "Poppy Spencer-Churchill. I have an appoint-ment." She winked at me and the aristocratic veneer instantly fell away.

The gate buzzed.

Poppy pushed it open and gestured for me to go first.

Without crowds milling around, it was even easier to appreciate the grandness of the building. The courtyard wouldn't have been out of place in the heart of old Paris. Inside, the echoes of our foot-steps bounced off marble floors and soaring marble-covered walls. Every direction held something beautiful or luxurious.

What was behind that set of grand doors? What was up those sweeping staircases? What other mysterious events were held here?

And did they need catering?

"Zelda?" Poppy's voice interrupted my thoughts.

I had stopped to gawk without even realizing it. "Coming," I said, jogging to catch up. I followed her out of the marble ballroom and into another room that would have held a decent-sized wedding reception. Instead of round banquet tables, though, chairs in rows faced a podium. Red velvet curtains hung over all the windows, leaving the room to be lit by yellow light from golden sconces along the walls. Red carpet covered the floor.

And above it all, the most over-the-top ceiling I'd ever seen in my life. There wasn't a square inch not completely covered in carvings, gilt, and paintings. Angels with torches and wheels. Horses on clouds surrounded by cherubs. Like an art museum exploded.

"Through here," Poppy said, indicating a side door.

I followed her.

The smaller door opened into a cozy library lit with similar sconces to the red velvet room. Four walls of dark wooden bookshelves framed a large rectangular table. A standing globe took up space off to the side along with a pair of wingback chairs. Old portraits hung above the bookshelves.

Then a section of the bookshelf swung open with a jingling noise—like the West Side Sandwiches door but much lighter—and a woman dressed in a blue and silver caftan emerged.

The bells I'd heard were the ones in her long twists of hair, along with other gems and silver charms. She was average height, but solid build. "Poppy!" she said, with arms outstretched.

Poppy bustled forward and embraced her. When they released each other, Poppy turned to me. "Azure, may I present my roommate Zelda Hawkins. Zelda, this is Azure Washington, Witch Presiding of the League of Women's Welfare."

"Or the Ladies Who Witch," Azure said. Her voice was almost gravelly, but pleasantly so, with a familiar New York accent. She aimed a smile in my direction. "We're all friends here."

I held my hand out. "Nice to meet you, Azure."

She held her hand out, then pulled it back. She nudged Poppy. "She doesn't actually *take* your magic, does she?"

Poppy fluttered her hands. "Oh, no. She just copies it."

"And only if I hold on for more than a second or two," I added.

Azure chuckled, then gave my hand a hearty shake. Her hand was strong and warm. "Pleased, I'm sure."

"Where's Aloysius?" Poppy asked.

"He's with my assistant."

"Aloysius is her familiar," Poppy added, to me. "He's an owl. Air magic familiar. Wings as big as tree branches." She turned to Azure. "Something happened to Zelda that was *almost* like a familiar—very strange—"

"Really?" Azure looked me up and down, as if reassessing.

I described what happened at the shop, from the griddle fire, to the appearance of the mouse, right up to the peeps, and then how I made the odd little creature disappear into my hand.

"Have you tried to summon it again?"

I shook my head.

"Interesting," Azure said. She peered over her gold-rimmed spectacles. "Let's have a look at you."

"What, here?"

"No, at Mount Sinai. Of course here, where did you think?" She shook her head with amusement, and her hair charms jingled. "Hands, please."

"If I touch you for more than a few seconds—"

"Yes, I know. That's what I want to see." She grasped my hands and turned them over like she might read both my palms.

I held still, expecting the cold swirl of air magic like my brother's. And it was, at first, a cool ticklish feeling accompanied by silver motes that stuck to my skin like glitter. But the temperature alternated, like a magical current, first cool, then warm, then cool again, not dissimilar to sitting in front of a fire while a door to the outside opens and closes repeatedly, causing the drafts to twine around each other. "I wonder why everyone's magic feels so different."

Azure raised her gaze briefly before returning it to my hands. "Why wouldn't it? If we were all the same, what a boring world it would be." She passed the pad of her thumb over my palm. "See this, Poppy? I think our magics are interacting. That's your fire magic, if I'm not mistaken."

Poppy leaned in and watched closer.

"Normally it takes a great amount of intention to transfer magic from one person to another. But here it is, hopping to your friend like fleas." Azure slid her hands up to my wrists, raising my arms higher. "Your grandmother was magical, Poppy said?"

"Yes. The same as me. She could copy magic, too."

"What about the rest of your family?"

"Mother and father, no. My brother, my maternal aunt and my cousin are all elemental witches."

"Type?"

"Air."

She released me. "Poppy, get a book."

Poppy hurried to the shelves and grabbed a book bound in tattered leather with gold lettering faded to the point of unreadability.

"Put it on the table and open it." Poppy did so. "Zelda, turn the pages with air magic."

I lifted my hand and sent drafts of air flying toward the book. Silver lines traced the air where they passed, then caressed the pages as they flipped over.

"Stop."

I lowered my hand. The pages fluttered one last time before going still, and the silver air magic disappeared.

"Conjure a fire in your hand."

I turned my hand palm-up and concentrated. A silver spark flickered, then a small yellow flame rose.

"Other hand, too."

I glanced at Poppy, who shrugged. I did as Azure asked.

"Malkin!" Azure called. "Bring me a candle, please."

A rustle of papers and a clatter came from beyond the open bookshelf door. "Coming, Azure," an unfamiliar voice replied.

Malkin emerged from the adjacent room. She was young, around Lily's age, twenty-something, with dark hair in a boyish cut, side-parted; a men's suit cut to fit; highly polished leather shoes; and an old-fashioned watch chain attached to a buttonhole on her vest. Dashing, like a modern Indiana Jones minus the hat. Malkin lifted a candle in a stone vessel. "Got it."

"Thank you. Put it on the table, away from the book. Poppy, you know Malkin. Zelda, this is Malkin. Assistant to the Witch Presiding."

Malkin raised a hand and gave me a casual salute.

"Malkin is a water witch. It helps to have one around if something goes wrong with fire."

"Why would something go wrong with fire?"

"Because I'm going to ask you to bring out that fire mouse of yours, and in case you hadn't noticed"—she gestured to the room—"we're in a library full of old and rare books. Now, I want you to concentrate on that candle. Specifically the wick. And I want you to think about that fire mouse you saw. Remember what it looked like. How it felt. What it sounded like. You're going to follow those feelings to wherever it went when it disappeared from your hand."

"And then what?"

"And then you're going to call it back. You're going to tempt it with this candle. With the wick. Fire *wants* something to burn, the same way you or I might want a snack after ten hours with no food."

I nodded. Azure was speaking my language.

"Hold your hand right next to the candle."

I stepped within reach of the candle, which looked oddly ordinary in the setting, and held out my hand. Malkin moved closer. "Can I close my eyes?" I asked.

"Whatever you need to do," Azure said.

I closed them.

There, in my mind's eye, was the fire mouse. It was crouched on its funny back legs, its front paws up, and its head was cocked, giving its oversized ears a quizzical tilt. Though it didn't make any particular sense, I pictured the fire mouse diving down the back of my neck and flying down my arm like a tiny roller coaster car to land in my palm. I pictured the unlit candle as its reward.

SNAP.

I opened my eyes at the sound. The whole top of the candle was burning, not just the wick, and the fire mouse was sitting in the melted wax.

"Ooh," Poppy said.

A ball of water floated over the candle. Malkin held both hands out, controlling it.

"Now what?" I asked.

"Hush," Azure said. She was feeding small streams of air toward the fire.

"If you give a mouse a cookie," I said, "he's going to ask for a glass of milk."

"Stop talking and think of a name."

"A name?"

"For the mouse. Name it."

I was not good at naming things. It had taken me ages to stop calling my dog "Boy" and settle on "Jester." And even then, it was only because it was so obvious that he was a clown.

"Fire Whiskers," Poppy said. "Or Fire Paws!"

"Fire-iana Grande," Malkin offered.

"No offense," I said, " but those are terrible." Meanwhile, the mouse had melted the wax all the way to the bottom.

Melt. The word conjured its own magic—that hot diner classic of hamburger, sauteed onions, and melted cheese on grilled bread. "Patty Melt!"

All three of them looked at me. No, four of them. Patty Melt, or Patty for short, turned her little mouse head in my direction, too.

"*Patty Melt*?" Azure said, her disbelief written in raised eyebrows.

"People who name their owls 'Aloysius' don't get to judge," I said.

I would have enjoyed delivering that retort even more if it hadn't been punctuated by a sudden, high-pitched, ungodly sound halfway between a hiss and shriek.

5

E veryone turned to look as a whirlwind of feathers blasted into the room. The owl banked at the corners and beat its wings to gain height.

"Aloysius, *no*," Azure said. Like you would say to a dog trying to counter-surf. Except this was no dog and it wasn't trying for crumbs.

It was a crazy-eyed owl after a mouse.

Patty Melt *peep*-ed and took off running across the table, leaving a thin trail of flames.

Malkin plunged the ball of water onto the candle, putting it out with a sudden hiss.

Aloysius dove.

I threw myself across the wooden table, knocking the wind right out of my lungs but managing to block the owl from reaching the fire mouse.

Aloysius wheeled away and landed on the globe, where he made disgruntled owl noises.

My ribs twinged. I was going to regret that hard landing in the morning. The fire mouse darted back and forth, looking for a place to hide, and I brought my arms closer, corralling her. "It's okay, Patty. I got you." I glanced over at Azure. "That owl under control yet?"

"When is magic ever truly under control?" Azure asked.

Malkin and Poppy were already working on the trail of flames. Malkin rolled the ball of water across the table, behind Poppy's pass, thoroughly squelching the fire after Poppy put it out.

"Not in the mood for philosophy," I said, scooping up Patty Melt. The mouse clung to her own tail and chittered like an angry customer.

Azure lifted Aloysius to her shoulder. "He forgot himself." She turned her head to meet the bird's demented gaze. "Isn't that right, my precious?"

Aloysius groomed her hair with gentle nips.

"We can all be a bit weird about our pets," Poppy said.

"That's a familiar, not a pet," I said, dragging myself off the table.

Azure smoothed the owl's feathers. "Pets, familiars. What's the difference?"

She had a point. Jester was as much a part of me as any witch's familiar. My soul outside my body. My little ball of stink, fluff, and love. I couldn't stay mad at him no matter what he did, not when he ate my socks, or destroyed the remote control, or shredded a roll of toilet paper all over our room.

Patty Melt yawned. Apparently being chased by a magical owl had worn her out. I lifted her up to the light. "But what's this gal? She's not a familiar, exactly. Is she?"

Azure started to approach, then stopped. "Malkin, take the King of the Air next door, will you? And shut the door."

"Will that stop him?" Poppy asked.

"Sort of," Azure said. She saw my face. "Mostly," she added. She handed the owl to Malkin, who retreated to the adjoining room and pulled the bookshelf door closed. Then Azure came closer and peered at the newly-christened fire mouse. "How often do you borrow magic?"

"Every day, when I can. Never hurts to stay fully charged. And Poppy and I are roommates, so it's easy."

Azure nodded. "Ever borrow any other kind? Air? Water? Earth?"

"Occasionally air magic, when my brother's in town."

"How often is that?"

"Every few months, I guess. Why?" Patty Melt had curled up in my palm and was now snoring like the world's tiniest motorboat.

"Did this happen to your grandmother, too?"

"Not that I know of..."

Azure plopped into a wingback chair and looked me up and down. "You're an odd one."

"Don't I know it."

She steepled her fingers. "Elemental magic tends to run in families. Often the same elemental magic. We also have witches—like

Poppy here—who seem to come out of nowhere. The key word here is *seem*. We have no way of really knowing what might be hiding on a remote branch of the family tree, probably because our ancestors weren't really keen on getting burned at the stake."

"Understandable," Poppy said.

Azure chuckled and removed her glasses. She polished them slowly on gathered material from her caftan. "I suspect that's the case with you, Zelda."

A prickle of cold ran down my spine. "What do you mean?"

"Somewhere in your family tree, there's something you don't know about. A secret kept hidden, now lost."

"Lost?"

"I propose that this new little friend of yours is a direct result of your borrowing fire magic from Poppy. I wouldn't be surprised if it isn't the last one, either."

"Isn't the last *what*?"

"The last creature to manifest for you."

I pulled out a chair and sat before I accidently dumped poor, sleeping Patty Melt onto the floor.

"Are you all right?" Poppy asked.

The sleeping mouse flamed softly like an old fire burning down to the coals. Hypnotic in its warmth and light. I let myself drift in it—reaching, reaching—into a past that remained behind a firmly locked door.

What was behind it?

Grandparents pass away. It's inevitable. Yet when they go, it's not just their love and presence that's missed. It's everything they experienced, everything they knew, all the tiny details that make up a life.

Gone. What we remember can be beautiful but can never, by definition, be complete.

"I'm all right," I said.

Poppy made a skeptical face. "You don't *sound* all right."

I carefully closed my other hand over Patty Melt. "Go to bed," I whispered. The warmth faded from its concentrated spot on my palm and spread through me until I could no longer feel it in any one place. It might not have been there at all but for the fact that I *knew* Patty Melt was still with me. I looked at the Witch Presiding. "Got any other surprises you want to drop on me while I'm here?"

Azure rested her chin in her hand and regarded me with an amused look. "I could say the same to you."

"Oh!" Poppy cried. "I forgot—I wanted to show you the statue. Come on." She gestured impatiently toward where we'd come in.

"What statue?"

"You'll see."

Azure Washington didn't stand, but her amused gaze tracked us as Poppy hustled me away. "Well met, Zelda Hawkins."

"Bye, Azure—oh, and if you hear the alarm, it's just us," Poppy added merrily. She dragged me back into the red-curtained ball-room.

"Alarm?"

"Don't worry. I have it totally under control."

Poppy had a lot of things, but *totally under control* wasn't one of them.

"I saw that." Poppy slapped me lightly on the arm. "Bad Zelda. For that, you must gallop twenty paces."

"I don't think that's a good idea in—" *Here*, I would have said, but she had already launched forward. I couldn't help but gallop along out of the meeting room and down a long hallway done up in creamy white, with gold accents everywhere: outlining the panels on the walls, covering the carved crown moldings. Even the light fixtures were gilded.

Our footsteps thumped on the plush carpet.

"Here we are," Poppy said, slightly out of breath as she came to a stop in front of a relatively unassuming-looking door.

It swung open to reveal a small landing followed by a semi-circular swirl of stairs with a white-columned railing. I peered down to the floor below, which was covered with a carpet that resembled a chambered nautilus. "Is this below street level?"

"Exactly," Poppy replied, leading the way. "That's why there are no windows. Better security, too," she added, turning and giving me a knowing wink.

We descended the stairs. Instead of windows, decorative panels stretched from floor to ceiling in between massive Greek columns. Each panel contained a painting of a woman wearing Greek robes, and sandals with laces.

A serious-looking woman in crimson robes held aloft a handful of fire as a crown of flames floated above her head. On the next panel, a woman in a rich brown cape cradled a white cat in front of a background of trees. White roses bloomed at her feet. Both the woman and the cat gazed out on the room knowingly. The next panel portrayed a dancing woman in blue, trailing a stream of sparkling water like a gymnast's ribbon. And finally, a woman in purple, standing on a cloud and surrounded by floating feathers.

Above it all, a blue sky ceiling with puffy white clouds.

"Who painted all this?" I asked, as we reached the lower level.

"It's a bit over-the-top, isn't it. I mean, really. Gold leaf, Greek columns, *and* floor-to-ceiling murals? Positively *shocking* taste." Poppy paused. "Kind of reminds me of home, when I think about it. Except home doesn't have one of those." She pointed up to a niche high up in the wall where a small statue stood.

You wouldn't notice it right away, thanks to the brightly-colored paintings, but once you actually saw it, it was hard to take your eyes off. It appeared to capture a dancer in a full-body veil, in the middle of a spin so gracefully shaped I almost expected the statue to swirl into motion at any moment. "Why's it up so high?"

"Because," Poppy said, with a mix of pride and relish, "it was *stolen*. And *I* got it back."

"You did?"

"I did indeed."

I regarded the statue again. It did have that strange attractive quality, but I couldn't see anything obvious about why it would be valuable, and I said as much to Poppy.

"Watch this." She held out her hands, and a small fireball popped in each palm.

Immediately, the statue began to stretch and sway.

I blinked. "Oh, wow—that's beautiful—" But I didn't have time to say anything else, because a hurricane force wind exploded out of nowhere. Like, the kind you have to lean into to stay upright. And then it was joined by a violently swirling white fog, rendering the room almost invisible as it tried to knock you down.

"Isn't it something?" Poppy yelled over the shrieking wind.

Chairs were falling over in every direction. Lighting fixtures threatened to rip free from the walls.

"Turn it off!" I yelled back.

The fire in Poppy's hands went out. The wind dropped, and although the fog hung around a few moments, it quickly dissipated. The dancing statue had stopped moving. "What the heck was that?"

"Security system," she said, finger-combing her hair back into place. "It goes off whenever magic is present."

"But you're a society of witches—why would you want that?" I didn't need to look to know that my own hair was a lost cause. Good thing I had a hat.

"You never know when you might want to keep people from using magic undetected. The statue senses magic," she added. "The security system was added after the theft, to prevent anyone from stealing it again."

"You could steal it without magic."

Poppy snorted. "How would you get up there? Fly?"

I put my hands on my hips, peered upward, estimated the distance. "I guess it *would* take a fireman's ladder."

"Exactly." She did a double take at me. "Don't get any ideas."

I laughed. "Why would I want a magical dancing statue?"

"You collect bits of magic without even trying. You're like some kind of magpie for magic."

Her hat had fallen under a table, so I grabbed it and jammed it onto her head. Crooked. "This magpie wants some lunch. What do you say we get out of here and hit that German place around the corner for bratwurst and pretzels?"

"Ooh, and potato pancakes and Black Forest cake!"

"And *spaetzle* with gravy."

Lost in a sparkling vision of German delights, Poppy danced up the stairs ahead of me.

I put my hand on the banister, then turned back for one last look. The subjects of the painting looked back at me. Witches of the elements. The dancing statue frozen, serene, above us all.

There were more mysteries at the League of Women's Welfare than could be solved in one visit.

6

By the time I finished my shift at the shop, the sun had slipped behind the buildings to the west. I could still see its orange glow down the streets that ran all the way to the Hudson River. I followed it until I reached the upper edge of Riverside Park—Berron's favorite hangout, where I'd promised to meet him at the fountain facing Riverside Drive.

The fountain was one of a handful of horse troughs built when horsepower still meant four legs. A stone eagle with wings spread perched on top of the fountain, its talons resting on oak leaves and acorns. A fanciful fish head spewed clean water into a stylized shell, where it then tumbled into a broad, shallow basin.

Berron was nowhere to be seen.

It was something I'd noticed about him. He wasn't there, until he suddenly was. Until he chose to let you notice him. Like he wore some kind of camouflage.

And then he was there, sitting casually on the low stone wall to the side of the fountain, smiling like he had a secret.

I sat next to him on the stone wall. "What are you grinning about?" I said, tilting my head back and attempting to fan away my sweat.

"Are you hot?"

"No, I just do this for fun."

He reached for my hand, but I instinctively leaned away. "Don't be ridiculous," he said. His words shouldn't have soothed me, but they did. I was no better than Jester, relaxing at his suggestion. Damn the Gentry and their understated magic.

He pried my hand away from where I'd crossed my arms, and wrapped it in his own hands. Gold magic and the scent of crisp leaves rippled between us. As the magic sank beneath my skin, delicious coolness filled me. I fought the urge to exhale with relief.

"Better?"

I nodded.

Satisfied, he returned my hand to the top of my leg and gave it a doctorly pat.

"Does that work for all temperatures?"

He tipped his head back, chuckled to himself. "How else would I sleep outside?"

"You sleep *outside*? You never told me that."

"You never asked."

"I thought you had some sort of apartment somewhere, filled with handmade wood furniture and pure linen sheets. Or something."

"I do. But I don't spend much time there. It's not home."

Home. Mine was Poppy's cheerful townhouse, but also a thousand miles away, in the funky Orlando neighborhood I'd left behind. How could such a simple four-letter word split your heart in two? And which spot claimed it more?

Berron didn't speak for a few moments. He shook his head, making a rueful twist of his lips. "I think I've been away too long."

"You visit all the time though, right? That's where that horse came from," I said, remembering the day of the opening party.

"Yes." He chafed his hands, though he couldn't have been cold. "But it's not the same. It's not enough. Not since—" He stopped. We both knew what he meant.

"How does the horse get along in there?"

"I bring her food. From outside. And she's never..." He paused, looking for the right words. "Fallen asleep. As it were."

"Is that what happened to your people?"

Berron nodded, his gaze troubled and distant.

I squeezed his arm. "I'm ready to go with you."

He turned and met my gaze, drinking in my intention, testing it like I would taste a batch of soup. "You're ready?"

"I arranged extra help at the shop. My aunt wanted to come up and visit Lily anyway—Lily's her granddaughter—and she'll step in as needed while I'm gone."

He looked genuinely surprised. "Your aunt? Here?"

"Why does that surprise you?"

He shrugged, possibly to cover the fact that he looked flustered. "They're so far away! Your family, I mean."

"Berron, I don't know if you know this, but they have these things called planes—"

"Just because I can't fly on them doesn't mean I don't know what they are, thank you very much."

Curiosity got the better of me. "What would happen if you did? Fly, I mean?"

"Ever heard of Sleeping Beauty? Well, that's what would happen, only no amount of kissing would wake me up."

Now *there* was a mental image. "Is it the same for the Blessed, if they try to leave Manhattan?"

"They remain awake, but suffer agonizing pain." He smiled at the thought.

"Harsh." I cleared my throat. "Speaking of the Blessed... how would you feel about Daniel coming with us?"

He laughed. "You're not serious." He looked at me. "You *are* serious." He pushed off the wall and paced next to the fountain. When he stopped, his tall frame was framed by the stone eagle wings, making him look like an angel. An avenging angel, considering the look on his face. "Why would I want someone like *him* tagging along? Bring Poppy, if you must. She's harmless."

"Poppy is not 'harmless.'" Even if Poppy was as harmless as a sleeping puppy, I wouldn't stand for anyone to dismiss her.

Berron waved his elegant hand. "You know what I mean." Then gave me a look laced with distaste. "Why do you want *Daniel* along, anyway?"

"Because," I said, pausing because I hadn't quite worked that part out, not entirely, anyway, other than an instinct that having Daniel and Poppy along *felt* like the right thing to do, "because he can help me maintain my energy—my strength—while we're there."

"Bah. Get him to top you up before you leave."

"It fades."

"We won't stay too long."

"How do you know that?"

He planted his hands on his hips, turned away. Then he turned on his heels and faced me again. "There is none of what he needs in my realm." *Blood*, he meant, without having to say it. "None that he's permitted to have, anyway."

"He doesn't need it that often."

Berron dropped into a crouch in front of me. "Zelda. Listen to me. My kind, his kind—we are the oldest of enemies. You can't ask this."

"I'm not asking it lightly."

He bowed his head, then looked up. "Please."

I reached for his hand and the magic spun between us again. With his great height folded before me, my words came out slower and gentler than they might have if he had towered over me. "You're relying on me to solve this mystery, to understand what happened to your home, because I have my grandmother's gift."

My thoughts became clear even as I spoke; what *felt* right had reasons behind it—and now I knew what they were. "But that gift isn't perfect. I can't do everything that Poppy can do. And I'm sure that you and Daniel have abilities that exceed mine. There may be something one of you can do, something one of you can see, that ends up being the key to solving this. I need all of you." I squeezed his hand. "Just because your kind and his kind are enemies doesn't mean that *you* and *he* have to be enemies."

Berron cocked his head and studied me for a long moment. "Oh, you sweet summer child."

"Get off," I said, rolling my eyes and releasing his hand with a backwards push.

He landed on his backside, laughing. "What?"

"Don't 'sweet summer child' me." I crossed my arms and turned away.

He was up and sitting on the wall next to me in a blink. "Ah, my Zelda—"

"Not your Zelda. And don't try to soothe me, or whatever it is you Gentry do."

"I wouldn't dream of it."

I snorted. "You probably do it without even thinking about it." I was still turned away, so he leaned in and rested his chin on my shoulder.

"Do I?" His warm breath tickled my cheek. "Is this soothing you?"

I pressed my lips together. How could anyone be so effortlessly exasperating? Yet my breath synced with his, and we gazed silently at the splashing fountain, in peace, as the last of the orange sunlight cast the eagle, the fish, and the carvings of leaves and acorns into shadow.

Stirring was like waking from a dream. "What will we need to bring with us?"

"You mean besides stout hearts and strong arms?"

I managed a smile. "Yeah."

"It's cooler there than it is here, now. You need warm clothing."

"I have that."

"Something that won't look out of place."

"What does *that* mean?"

He plucked at the frayed hem of my cutoffs. "Something that looks like you belong with the Gentry. Natural fibers, too."

I remembered that day at the Mirror, when Berron had appeared dressed as a Gentry prince, all warm browns and greens, accented with gold, the very picture of forest royalty. "Why does it matter, if everyone's asleep?"

"The goal is for them not to be. And—to be honest—man-made fabrics *smell*."

I sat up straight, which forced him to do the same, and gave him a look. "They *smell*?"

"Not a lot, mind you, but yes. They do."

"How about my man-made underpants? Those okay?" I asked, sarcasm at full strength.

"I wouldn't dream of criticizing someone's"—he cleared his throat—"personal items."

I laughed. "Poor Prince. Can't even say 'underpants.' Some smooth talker you are."

"I can say it. I was only trying to be respectful." He hunched up and looked for all the world like an oversized, offended cat. "If my people smell something offensive in their sleep, they may have nightmares—and no way to wake up from them."

Well, slap me with a cold cut. I wasn't going to give a bunch of innocent Gentry bad dreams just because I like rayon undies. "Hey," I said, giving Berron's shoulder a little shake, to make the point. "No nightmares. No problem." Then a thought occurred to me: how would I get Poppy and Daniel to go along with it? Poppy would be agreeable, that was her nature, but Daniel...

"You're frowning," Berron said.

"Am I?"

"What's wrong?"

"It's kind of a big ask to make Poppy and Daniel buy new clothes just to fit in."

"Why? They're both rich."

I punched him in the arm. "You're being demanding."

"Am I?" he said, all innocence.

I shot him a look, and he pretended to duck and cover.

"All right," he said, stifling a laugh. "I'll pay for it. In fact, why don't you get your cousin to make us a few things? Didn't you say she sewed, and she needed money?"

"How am I going to explain to Lily why we need matching outfits made for a trip we can't talk about?"

"They don't have to *match*." He made a face of disgust. "Ugh. Matching with *Daniel*."

"You know what I mean."

"You just have to smell less human—and look more Gentry, in case everyone wakes up," he added, hopefully. Then he stood, pivoted to face Riverside Park, and surveyed the trees below like they were his very own domain. A mischievous smile slid across his face. "I think I have an idea."

7

Lily leaned on the drafting table and peered at the four of us. Her oversized cream-colored sweater bunched on her arms where she'd pushed up the sleeves, and the hem landed just above where her black skirt ended. Black tights and cute black boots completed the casually stylish NYU fashion student look, and the icy air conditioning in the studio made the heavier clothing make sense for high summer.

Behind her, clothing racks lined part of the wall, holding dozens of pieces in a riot of colors and fabrics. Bins filled with notions were arranged on a nearby table. A single large window provided natural light and the view to the street, several stories below. Sketches covered Lily's table and a large cork board, concepts for everything from great sweeping dresses to trim-looking blazers and everything in between. "Let me get this straight," she said. "You're going to put on a *show*?"

"Yes," I said, taking the lead because Poppy seemed to be wide-eyed at the whole concept of lying, Daniel had gone stone-faced, and Berron had wandered off and begun pawing through a bin full of feathers. "*A Midsummer Night's Dream*."

"Don't you need more than four people?"

Lily had an inquisitive side I hadn't accounted for. "We're just filling in the minor fairy roles." I turned. "Berron!"

The fairy prince looked up from the feather bin. "Yes?" He blew away a feather that had stuck to his lips.

"What were they called again?"

"Peaseblossom, Cobweb, Moth, and Mustardseed."

I turned back to Lily. "Right. Those."

"Mm-hm," she said, giving the four of us another once over before pulling out a notebook, flipping it open, and jotting something down. "And this production is at a theater...?"

"A charity show!" volunteered Poppy. She beamed at her own improvisation, and appeared to barely avoid a triumphant wink in my direction.

That got another look from Lily. "A charity show."

I nodded, wordlessly.

"Which of you is playing which fairy?"

"I'm not Peaseblossom," Daniel said, raising one finger in the air for emphasis.

Everyone looked at him.

"Just saying," he added, with a shrug of his muscular shoulders.

"It doesn't matter which one you are," I snapped.

"It does, though," Lily said, tapping a pencil on her chin thoughtfully. "I mean, that's how we'll pick colors, silhouettes, and so on."

"I'm not Peaseblossom," muttered Daniel.

I landed an elbow in his side. "You'll be whatever I say, and you'll like it," I said, for his ears only.

Berron abandoned the feather bucket and sauntered forward. "I'll be Peaseblossom." He looked at Daniel and smirked.

Lily was scrolling through her phone. She glanced up at Berron. "Purple's not your color."

Berron looked like he'd been shot. "But—I *like* purple..."

Daniel suppressed a laugh.

But Lily had gone back to scrolling, and hadn't noticed a thing. The four of us stood quietly while she tapped and swiped. Then she set her phone down with a thump. "According to tradition, Peaseblossom is purple. Mustardseed, obviously, is yellow. Cobweb is black and white. Moth—well, there's more flexibility there." She got up, approached Daniel first. Her small hands landed on his shoulders and turned him around with surprising force for her smaller stature. She faced him forward again, looked him up and down with a professional eye. "You're Cobweb." She walked around him, slowly, with a businesslike look on her face. "Cobwebs staunch blood. I'm sure we can do something with that."

My heart skipped a beat. Daniel caught my eye, clearly rattled.

Lily stepped to Poppy, took her hands, extended Poppy's arms out to the side, and spun her like an open umbrella.

"Oh, my," Poppy said, coming to a stop with a wobble.

Lily cocked her head. "You're Mustardseed. Mustardseed provides heat. I think we can do something with colors, to communicate that."

Poppy's mouth opened and closed. We barely had time to trade glances before Lily moved in front of me.

This was my cousin's daughter. Someone I'd known as a sweet kid with celiac disease, a young woman with big New York dreams, and now a crackerjack worker on my restaurant's front line. Yet with her clear blue eyes on me, a tremor went through me.

She hasn't shown any magic, I reminded myself.

Yet, the treacherous side of my mind added.

"Peaseblossom is purple," Lily said, turning me around. "It's considered almost as powerful a love potion as the one they use in the story. He's not Peaseblossom," she continued, nodding to Berron. She stopped turning me but the room kept on spinning. "You are."

I forced a laugh. Big mistake, as it knocked the air out of my lungs. "You know me, such a love-hound."

"Something in dreamy purples," Lily said, in complete seriousness.

Daniel and Berron stared at me, just long enough for Lily to move to Berron.

"You're different," she said.

Berron's self-possession animated him like an espresso. "I like to think so."

Though he was older, taller, and appeared so confident it was almost intimidating, Lily was unfazed. She walked around him.

"Moths were sacrificed to make medicine, generally by being smoth-ered in rose petals."

He tried to track her movement as she circled him. "Maybe not different like *that*—"

"You're Moth," Lily said, coming to a stop. She didn't ask if we approved of her selection of roles. "I think I can work with that. It's okay if it's simple, right, Zelda?"

"Simple is great," I said, still trying to put together what she'd seen in each of us to pair us with our roles. "Something that can be put together in a few days."

Lily returned to the drafting table and leaned over her notebook. "Simple design, natural fibers. Cobweb, Mustardseed, Peaseblos-som, and Moth."

"And it's cold," I added.

Lily looked up. "It's summer, Aunt Zelda."

"I mean in the building where we're doing the charity show," I said. "So it would be good for the costume itself to be warm. Like long sleeves, or a cape or something."

"Capes," Lily said, scribbling it down.

"Ooh, capes!" Poppy said, clapping her hands.

Lily speared the pencil into a cup, where it clattered around be-fore coming to rest. "Let's get you measured." She scooped up a pink tape measure and began taking measurements—across my shoulders, around the bicep, down the arm, and so on—making notes as she went. After I was done, she did Poppy, then Daniel, both of whom seemed familiar with the process, and finally Berron, who seemed vaguely amused by it. "That's all of them," she said. "Now, about the fabric. You said natural fibers? What kind?"

"What kind?" I echoed.

"You have your plant fibers, like cotton and linen, and your animal fibers, like wool, cashmere, silk..." She looked at me expectantly.

I looked to Berron for help, but Daniel answered first. "Mid-weight wool for slacks, cashmere-silk blend for tops, and for the capes—" He unexpectedly turned to Berron. "Water-resistant wool?"

Berron gave Daniel a slight bow. "As you say."

"Water-resistant wool," Lily repeated, writing it down. "Are you okay with me picking everything out?"

"Go crazy," I said.

"How crazy? What kind of budget are we working with?"

"I'll cover it," Berron said, just as Daniel said, "Whatever you need." By carefully not looking in each other's direction, they managed to pretend the other hadn't spoken.

"And whatever payment is fair for your work," I added. "And your friends," I said, thinking of the other fashion design students who had been at that children's party at Victorine's house. "If it would help to have extra pairs of hands to get it done."

"This must be some charity event," Lily said, finally smiling.

"Oh, it *is*," Poppy said.

"I'd love to see your show—"

"Oh, *no*," Poppy said, quickly changing her tone. "They want five *thousand* dollars a head."

"Well, take lots of pictures for me, then. And maybe a video!" she added brightly.

"Definitely," Berron said. He had found a length of Scottish tartan and had wrapped it around his waist like a kilt. "I hear your grandmother's coming for a visit?"

Lily's gaze went to me briefly before she replied. "She is. She hasn't been here in many years, so she's eager to see the city, do the tourist things."

"That's very exciting. Family is so important."

"Yes, it is," I agreed, wondering why he was leading the conversation in that direction. "But we should let Lily get on with it, so..."

"Thank you very much," Daniel said to Lily, holding his hand out to shake.

"Ta-ta!" Polly said brightly, waggling her fingertips.

"Goodbye, Zelda's cousin," Berron said, nodding politely before returning the tartan to its place.

Downstairs, I snagged Berron. "When did you get so curious about Lily and Aunt Belinda?"

"Her name is Belinda?" he asked, with the air of someone filing the information away for later.

I was about to respond when I noticed Daniel slipping out the door. "Daniel! Wait up."

His whole body came to a stop like he'd discovered the door was in fact a wall. He turned to face me.

Berron and Poppy looked on.

"Are you going somewhere?"

"Yeah, I was going to go catch a show."

Every face has its microexpressions. When you know someone for long enough, you get to recognize them. In this case, it was Daniel's eyes. They weren't blinking. They held my gaze too steadily, as if he was willing himself not to waver. Then, in a tiny movement completely out of its natural rhythm, he blinked.

That was all it took. *Blink.*

This was how we lied to one another: mirrored poker faces. His, to hide the lie. Mine, to hide the fact that I knew.

"Oh," I said, relaxing into a fake smile. "Want company?"

"I'd love it," he lied. "But it's sold out."

"Bummer." I punched his arm lightly. "Have fun." I let him slip out the door, slip away into the heat, knowing he wasn't going where he said he was going. I turned to Poppy. "I'll see you back at home, okay? I have to run an errand." The lie rolled off my tongue and I was out the door before either of them could stop me, following Daniel into the streets of New York.

8

He couldn't know I was following him, yet if all he had to do was turn his head to see me, I wasn't going to be able to follow him for long. If I ducked into a phone booth to disguise myself—if phone booths existed anymore, which they didn't—I'd lose him.

Thoughts of home, of Jester and Georgiana, of relaxation and whatever chocolate treat Poppy would surely pick up on the way there, whispered *Walk away, Zelda.*

Another instinct, the one that didn't so much as dislike getting lied to as it disliked the idea of not catching it and rubbing it in the other person's face, well—that instinct snarled its way through my body and kept me stalking.

But how to do it without getting caught?

The crowds flashed by on the sidewalk like schools of fish, always pointed in one direction or another, opening and closing ranks with the tides. Except these fish followed the unwritten code of the city: *never make eye contact.* No matter what. Do anything short of falling to the ground, and New Yorkers would look past you as if you didn't exist.

My hand went to my face instinctively, as if checking if the magical mask granted by the Arcade was still there. Of course it was. It had never budged from my face, although I'd found few opportunities to use it. Didn't mean I hadn't practiced, though. In the privacy of my own room, I'd amused myself with hundreds of disguises.

Daniel, with his long stride, was outpacing me.

My face would give me away if I didn't hurry up and disguise myself.

I had to time it just right. And faces were tricky. You couldn't just pick someone you knew, or even someone you once saw in the street. Those could backfire. Celebrity faces were easy to imagine, but would mean unwanted attention or even getting mobbed. My younger face, which I'd used once before, was off limits. Daniel would easily recognize it.

It had taken me a while to figure out a solution for faces. I found it while browsing a used bookstore: vintage copies of *Good Housekeeping* magazine. The old ads for dishwashers and eye creams were full of faces, clearly photographed, and not typically famous enough to be recognizable to anyone. I brought home an armful of magazines and carefully memorized my favorites of the anonymous faces within. From time to time I'd take them out and study them again to make sure the memory stayed clear.

I turned, hid my face in the crook of my arm, and let out my best imitation of a sneeze. Diamond strands of magic blasted out of the mask and swirled over my face. I was prepared for the flash of glittering light, for the prismatic, sparkling moment of change. I lifted my head and fast-walked after Daniel. He'd never recognize the face of a woman from a 1960s ad for detergent.

I grabbed my hair with both hands as if pulling it back into a ponytail. What I was really doing was making it temporarily hidden while I altered it. Again the light and the white rainbow of colors, this time streaking back over my hands and my hair. When the magic dimmed and I released my hair, I knew that to any onlooker, it was now pixie-cut auburn instead of medium-length black streaked with gray.

My clothing I changed a shade at a time, an inch at a time, slow pulses of swirling magic sliding down my body, turning the shirt into something lighter and longer until it looked completely different from the black tank I really had on. Then my shorts. Then my shoes. Daniel had an eye for clothing and I couldn't take even the slightest risk of him seeing something recognizable.

Different face, check.

Different hair, check.

Different clothing, check.

Daniel would never see me coming.

I silently thanked whatever higher power was listening that Daniel didn't take cabs or public transportation unless he had to. He had a certain amount of pride in walking. I think he liked to show off his health, even if it was only to himself. How did that feel now that he had become a vampire of nearly inexhaustible strength and stamina? Did he miss earning his fitness? Or did he move comfortably in his newfound power like it was one of his custom-made suits?

I sped up. We crossed the intersections together, side by side sometimes, two strangers who weren't. We passed through the theater district and entered the neighborhood known as Hell's Kitchen.

Where are you going, Daniel?

Once a place of gangs and crime, Hell's Kitchen had gentrified to the point where billionaires bought condos they didn't use overlooking oversized sculptures with less artistic value than what the Central Park horses left behind. But if you ignored the new and the sleek and the glossy, the neighborhood had its charms: tiny family-run storefronts, hole-in-the-wall restaurants, old residential buildings built on a shorter scale, only a few stories high, with zigzagging fire escapes down the front.

It was into one of those little restaurants that Daniel ducked, a Puerto Rican place with a huge photo of mofongo on the window. The scent of garlic and oil spun out into the street when he opened the door.

I followed.

The restaurant was brightly lit, with huge menu boards above the counter, all red, white, and blue themed, with more color photos: pork, chicken or shrimp mofongo; sweet plantains; tres leches cake; Malta soda.

Daniel had taken a seat. A waitress approached, but he told her to come back in a few minutes.

I took a seat as close as I could without being conspicuous. I picked up a laminated menu off the table and pretended to look it over as I watched him. He was as calm as ever. How could he be that calm if he was up to something?

A seed of doubt grew like a time-lapse weed. Maybe he had just wanted to be left alone to eat a large pile of Puerto Rican food. Maybe he had ditched me to avoid stunning me with mofongo garlic breath.

The door swung open—

And it was as if a punch landed square in my chest.

Jessica. The vampire who bit him, sent him hurtling toward death, from which he could only be saved by being turned himself. Smug little face beneath a dark bob and equally dark sunglasses. Tight t-shirt. Short, pleated skirt. Knee-high boots.

And Daniel stood up for her. Pulled out a *chair* for her.

Air-kissed her cheek.

My blood felt like it was draining away onto the floor.

A waitress cut off my view. "What can I get you?"

I had a sudden urge to tell this stranger what I had just witnessed. Instead, I swallowed over a dry mouth and quickly read the menu for real. "Uh... half chicken, yellow rice, red beans. For here. And another one packed up to go."

"Anything to drink?"

I set down the menu, still in shock, my gaze drawn to the two-top of Daniel and the woman who nearly killed him. "Coke."

She nodded, and started to turn away.

"Oh, and two flans to go." My appetite ran on autopilot and ordered dessert even in the middle of a crisis.

The waitress left.

How could I not stare at the two of them? Talking like—well, not quite like old friends, but like this wasn't their first time getting together. I forced my gaze away and imagined my ears going up, like Jester's, to catch every word.

If my anxious breath didn't give me away first.

"I was afraid you wouldn't come," Jessica said.

Daniel's hand ghosted over the side of his neck before he responded. "Why wouldn't I?"

Jessica giggled. It was hard to square the fact that she looked so young with what I knew about her age, which was close to mine. Giggling just isn't very forty-ish.

Her fingers danced across the table like spiders. "Some people would think I'm scary." She wiggled her fingers at Daniel, then withdrew her hands.

Daniel smirked. "Try harder."

Her eyelids lowered, as if in false modesty. "Not here."

Were they *flirting*? What the *hell* was going on here? Immediately I thought of Poppy, and wondered if she'd seen anything in Daniel's thoughts during the fitting, or on his way out the door.

The waitress came to their table and took their order: French fries for Jessica, flan for Daniel.

I stifled a frown. That was a pitiful order for taking up space at a table. As I could have guessed, though, neither one touched the food when it was delivered.

I nibbled at my chicken and rice, enough to look occupied but not enough to have to actually deal with too much food in my flip-flopping stomach.

"So what did he say?" Daniel asked.

"He's intrigued," Jessica said. "He wants to know more."

"I want to talk to him directly."

"Oh, I don't think we're at that stage yet..."

Daniel stood. "Then we have nothing else to discuss."

Her fingers wrapped around his wrist. "Patience, Daniel."

His gaze slid to her grip, held it like the look alone would break each and every one of her fingers. "Some people would think I'm scary," he said, simply, without heat.

Fear—real fear—flickered in her eyes, swiftly covered by a cocky smile. She released his wrist, but let her fingers tickle his hand before she moved it away entirely. "Try harder." The comeback would have sounded better if her voice hadn't wobbled.

His gaze left her, moved around the room, as if taking in the very normal setting of tables and chairs, colorful signs, soda bottles, and anonymous patrons.

Like me.

He looked at Jessica. "Maybe I will. But not here."

If I were her, I wouldn't have known whether to feel threatened, flirted with, or some unholy mix of both. Then I realized I was staring at Daniel with something like admiration, and had to make myself look away.

"Set up a real meeting," Daniel said. And he left, leaving the flan behind, untouched, quivering.

I could have followed him. Could have confronted him, even. But I wasn't ready for that. I needed time to think. Time to plan.

Meanwhile, Jessica stared into her wax paper-lined basket of fries as if it were a crystal ball.

There was a bottle of ketchup on my table. I picked it up, weighed it in my hand, flipped it once. Then I leaned toward Jessica, bottle extended. "Need ketchup?"

She looked up, startled. "What?"

"Do you need ketchup?" I waggled the bottle. "You can have mine. I'm not using it."

"Oh." She took it, listlessly, and set it on her own table. All the energy she'd brought to her exchange with Daniel had evaporated, leaving her looking tired, the thick black liner around her eyes less a seduction than an echo of the dark circles beneath.

I'd promised myself to kill this woman, but she looked half-dead already.

Jessica stood and abruptly picked up the basket and the ketchup bottle. "Here." She plunked them on my table as if she hardly knew what she was doing, or why. "You have them. I'm not hungry." And with that, she was gone, out the door and into the streets of Hell's Kitchen.

I watched her leave.

Then I scooped up my mortal enemy's French fries, to go.

9

J ester bolted to the front window and stood on his hind legs with his front paws on the windowsill, as if he were a very small man. His crisp bark echoed through the townhouse. He turned his fuzzy head and looked at me, a very familiar look that said: *Mama! Mama! There's someone outside!*

"Of course there is, boy. It's Aunt Belinda." Jester downgraded his bark to a dubious grumble, and I went to the window. A yellow cab had stopped just outside.

When the car door opened, Jester whined loud and long. This was the noise he made when he changed tactics from world's most ridiculous watchdog to world's fuzziest welcoming committee. He pawed at the glass, making sounds that veered between peeping, whining, and yelping.

"Settle down," I said, attempting to smooth my hand down his back.

He danced sideways on two legs, like a circus poodle—then bolted for the door.

"Jester!" I ran after him.

He leaped at the door like a dog possessed.

I lunged for his harness and managed to snag him. Then I scooped him up into my arms like he was a little black sheep. He wiggled but calmed down enough so that I could open the door.

And there, on the front step, stood Belinda Campbell. My mother's sister. The mother of my cousin Luella, and grandmother of Luella's daughter, Lily.

Although she had to be in her late sixties or early seventies, she gave off an air of wiry vitality. Silver-white hair pulled tightly back in a bun. Long skinny legs in cutoff jean shorts, like mine, but much shorter. Beat-up white sneakers and no visible socks. A black Bike Week tank top. Sunglasses so burned out you could see the plastic peeling away from the lenses. "Zelda, girl! How you been? Ain't seen you in an age!"

"Aunt Belinda!" I tried to hug her with one arm, but Jester went wild, scrabbling frantically to get to the new person whose face needed to be kissed.

"And who's this handsome lil' gentleman?"

"This is Jester, and he"—the handsome lil' gentleman somehow managed to kick me right in the face in his attempt to get free—"he's a little overexcited right now."

"Aw, that's all right. I love dogs." She hauled her suitcases across the threshold with surprising strength, then shut the door. "Lemme hold him."

Jester's legs were almost a cartoon blur as he attempted to run on air to get to Aunt Belinda. She lifted him to her shoulder like he was a baby, and he gratefully licked her ear. "Ain't he precious," she said.

"Do you have a dog at home?"

"Me? Naw. I ain't gonna drop dead and leave a poor dog behind. My Luella, she got enough to keep up with." Aunt Belinda cackled. "But I love me a good hound." She nuzzled the curly fur at the nape of Jester's neck, and he returned the favor by attempting to remove her hair scrunchie, very delicately, with his teeth. Then she walked further into the room, still carrying Jester like a baby on her shoulder. "This where I'm gonna stay?"

I blinked. "On the couch?"

"Y'all ain't got but two bedrooms, right?"

"Well, yeah, but I figured you'd want to stay in a hotel—"

"Pshaw. Put a couple of blankets on here and I'm as right as rain. These old bones can sleep anywhere." She lofted Jester and looked right in his eyes. "Ain't that right, Mr. Poodle?"

He licked her nose.

Aunt Belinda peeked around my shoulder like I was hiding something. "Now where's my grandchild? Where's Lily?"

"She's in class today."

Aunt Belinda snorted. "I gotta make sure she's eatin' right. Girl could get blown over in a stiff wind."

"She looked fine when I saw her—"

"And all these big city witches around, too. I don't trust 'em. What else you got around here?"

"What else of what?"

"*You* know," she said. "Funny business. Paranormal stuff."

"Well, there's the Blessed..."

"Them's the vampires that can't leave?"

I nodded. "And the Gentry..."

"Fairies," she muttered, shaking her head. "Can't trust none of them, neither. Your mama said you had something real important to do up here. What is it?"

She had dropped everything to come up and help without knowing any of the details. Now that she was here, it was time to tell her the full story. So, once I had settled her on the couch and Jester distracted with a rolling ball that dispensed kibble, I started all the way at the beginning. The birthday party and Victorine. Berron and the restaurant. My witchy roommate, Poppy. Daniel and the vampires. Azure and the Ladies Who Witch. The Mirror Seal and the dying realm of the Gentry.

I left out Daniel's mofongo meeting.

"Shoot, girl," Aunt Belinda said, when I was finished. "You been right busy." She frowned, and wrinkles traced across her forehead. "Lily ain't involved in none of this?"

"No." I swallowed. That wasn't strictly true. "Well, actually, she's making some clothing for us. I forgot that part."

Her gaze sharpened into the distance, as if seeing something far away. "Girl's gotta finish her schooling."

"Believe me, I understand. She doesn't know about any of us." I couldn't bring myself to share Lily's uncanny assignment of roles to

Berron, Daniel, Poppy, and me. Not yet. Not without real evidence. "I mean, it wouldn't be *bad* though—if she turned out to be a witch?"

Her smile made wrinkles appear around her ice-blue eyes. "Heck, Zelda. My mama was a witch. I'm a witch. My only child is a witch. I ain't scared of witchery. But Lily ain't got nobody here to protect her."

"I'm here," I said, vaguely insulted that I didn't qualify as Lily's protector.

"Of course you are, girl. You got your hands full though, don't you, what with looking after the restaurant and the Mirror and all those Gentries and such. And now you're going someplace we don't know nothing about." She laced her fingers behind her head and leaned back. "I mean, *someone* may know about it, but that's the trouble with us witches being cut off from one another. You got witches in one city, witches in another city, and they can't call each other on the telephone, or send an email or nothing, for fear of being exposed. You got no idea what's going on anywhere else." She paused. "Sometimes I wish it weren't a secret no more."

"Didn't your mom ever talk to you about anything? About the Mirror? Or anything else?"

Aunt Belinda shook her head slowly. "I think she was protecting us. Kinda like how I never told Luella a thing till she was over forty and magical herself." She paused, as if lost in thought. Then she sat up and thumped her hands on the couch cushions, once, like gavels bringing a court to order. "Right. I'm gonna take care of things on this end, don't you worry. You go fix those fairies. And Lily can take me to see the Statue of Liberty and so on. I ain't leaving till I've had the full New York experience."

"Pace yourself," I said. "It's a different kind of heat than what you're used to."

She laughed. "I'm tougher than the Devil and twice as mean. Ain't no New York weather gonna stop me."

There was a scrabbling noise outside—the telltale sound of Georgiana's massive paws coming up the steps. "And there's Poppy now." I got up and opened the door for the two of them.

Poppy entered and peered at Aunt Belinda like she was a new addition to the Central Park Zoo. "Is this your aunt?"

I nodded.

"Oh, how *lovely*! An aunt of Zelda! And you're a witch?" she added, without waiting for an answer. "How perfectly marvelous!" She bustled over with Georgiana and held out her hand. "Very pleased to meet you. I'm Poppy Spencer-Churchill, Zelda's roommate."

"You're the fire witch, then," Aunt Belinda said, shaking the extended hand. "Belinda Campbell."

Poppy was smiling and shaking hands when suddenly she let go and drew back with a look of concern. "Does she know...?" She made an odd gesture, like flashbulb pops, around her own head.

Her mind-reading, of course. I hurried to explain. "Aunt Belinda, Poppy's fire magic comes with mind-reading, and she can't turn it off. When she's within about six feet of you, she can see little pictures of what you're thinking about. She likes to be upfront about it, at least with magical people."

"Well, I'll be darned," Aunt Belinda said. "That's right strange. Never heard of it being uncontrollable before." She cocked her head and looked Poppy up and down before nodding once, decisively. "I ain't worried. If I'm gonna think something rude, I'll step back a few paces." She winked at Poppy.

Poppy smiled with relief. "That's very kind of you, Mrs. Campbell."

"Ain't nobody calls me that, child. You just call me Mama."

Georgiana, freed from her leash, accepted a scritchy-scratch from Aunt Belinda, then ambled after the kibble toy Jester was chasing.

There was something cozy about having Aunt Belinda here. Seeing her and Lily made me miss my mom, though Mom and Aunt Belinda were as different as sweet tea and hot sauce. I even missed Bruce, a little. It was like we were all different pieces of the same puzzle.

Jester paused wrestling with the kibble ball, and peered at me with his head cocked and ears lifted as if I'd said something aloud.

I hadn't, but his curious gaze encouraged me to speak. Or maybe it was the sound of my grandmother chuckling to herself in the great beyond. "Hey, Aunt Belinda," I said, easing into one of the side chairs. "What do you think about having a family reunion someday?"

She and Poppy were comparing elemental spells, sending swirls of air and tiny fireworks around the room. Aunt Belinda clenched her casting hand neatly, bringing the breeze to a stop. "Why, Zelda girl," she said. "I think that might just be a *marvelous* idea!"

10

There's terror and joy when you realize you can't walk away. I felt both as I faced the Mirror Seal in my new threads. The wavy, smoky glass reflected flowing pants in eggplant, an flower-embroidered vest in an amethyst shade over a whisper-soft lavender sweater, and, in the same color as the pants, a lightweight cape with a hood. Lily had turned Peaseblossom into a character that wouldn't have been out of place sneaking across roofs, robed in purple shadows like a thief at late sunset.

Poppy, as Mustardseed, had been fitted with a long-sleeved buttercup yellow tunic and shamrock green slacks. Instead of a vest, a wide fabric belt embroidered with mustard flowers provided definition. Her cape was also shamrock green, although the hood lining was yellow. The color combination highlighted her eyes, which were wide with wonder and anticipation as we stood before the Mirror.

The fabric Lily had chosen for Daniel's clothing was black, shot through with faint and wriggling threads of white like he'd walked through a thousand cobwebs. This spidery fabric made up his tailored slacks, vest, and coat; a solid black fabric for his collared dress shirt. The only color was the cape lining in blood red. It made the red in his eyes even more gem-like. Inhuman.

But still gorgeous, whether I trusted him or not.

I couldn't think about that now, not when I had to concentrate. Instead, I nudged Berron. "You could have provided your own costume, you know."

"Where's the fun in that?" He raised his arms and turned, slowly, enjoying the attention.

His clothing, on the day he revealed who he was, was far more what I would have imagined to be "Gentry." All brown and green and gold, Robin Hood and Renaissance fairs, unsurprising and *safe*, in a way. But this...

This was different.

In a way it was the opposite of Daniel's outfit. The underlying color was white: creamy white slacks, white greatcoat. Layers of fluttering, wing-like capes crowned the shoulder of the coat. The piping along the edges was black, in contrast, and the slacks had black piping down the outside seams. Lily had affixed something like a moth wing's eyespots to the back of the greatcoat, so that when Berron turned away, he seemed to be looking at you still.

How like him. Always, always watching. I had to remind myself: No matter how young, how human he appeared to be, Berron was far older and *other* than any of us.

He caught me staring, and smiled. "Do you like it?"

"It's perfect." It was. It was a perfect reminder to be on my guard, to take nothing for granted. And I wondered if, on some level,

Lily was sending me that message whether or not she understood it herself.

I got closer to the Mirror. It was the same as I remembered it. Workmanship that rivaled anything in a museum. Carved birds and sparkling crystals, twisting vines and branches entwined. I laid a hand on the frame, brought my face close to the clouded silver surface. It was here that Poppy had seen a vision of the original enchantment, of the coming together of witch and vampire and fae magic that sealed the peace. The peace I had slashed open with my new chef's knife, to stop Lord Prospero. To save a dying realm. To uphold my grandmother's legacy.

Everything in my body drew me forward, threatened to pitch me forward through the Mirror and into the beyond. "Let's go," I said.

Before I lost my nerve.

Berron approached, drew me away from the silvery surface, positioned himself first. He held out his hand.

I took it, meeting his gaze with what I hoped was determination. Then I reached back for Poppy's hand. Fire magic swirled into one hand and Gentry magic into the other. The combination was dizzying.

Poppy took Daniel's hand. Chained together, we followed Berron, who stepped over the bottom part of the frame and into the Mirror itself. The silver fog swallowed up his foot, then his leg, and finally the rest of his body as he moved all the way through.

I stumbled a little, though he had moved slowly, and clasped his now-disembodied hand as I lifted my foot over the frame. There was a resistance, not of force, but of sensation, like cold air billowing out of a walk-in freezer. My leg slid into the cold and my heart skipped a beat as momentum took me the rest of the way.

My foot struck the ground on the other side, found it solid. Then the other foot.

I was through.

Around me, trees soared to heights I'd never seen before except in pictures. Sickly green light filtered from a sky hidden by leaves and lit only with flashes of golden heat lightning. Only oncoming hurricanes had ever given me such a sense of unease. A sky crawling with power. The air itself telling you something's wrong.

Berron still had my hand. "Don't be afraid," he said.

I needed to deliver a comeback, something to show I hadn't been rattled, but the words died in my chest and I had to remember to close my open mouth.

"The others," he murmured.

"Right." I was still holding Poppy's hand. Berron let go of mine and I turned fully to face where I'd come from.

The Mirror was exactly the same on both sides.

Before I had time to really marvel, Poppy came through. "Ooh," she said, stopping immediately in front of the Mirror, letting go of my hand, and letting her gaze travel over the forest.

"Watch out for Daniel," I said.

Poppy turned to face the Mirror and used her free hand to stabilize Daniel's arm.

Daniel emerged, wary, his brows coming together as he took in the strange environment. "Nice place you have here."

Berron's half-smile could have sliced a tomato. "Thank you, Daniel. I'm sure when your world dies, I'll have a similar remark for you." In the sad green light his costume looked even more surreal, startlingly white-gold when the lightning flashed, a canvas for the underwater green when it didn't.

"We won't let it die," I said. "That's why we're here." I knelt, touched the grass. It was cool and dry, but supple. It wasn't dead, at least not in the way the grass in Florida turned brown and crispy during a drought, but the color had faded like cut herbs left in the refrigerator too long. "Does it grow?"

"It's asleep," said Berron. "Like everything else."

"Is it supposed to be this color?" I gestured to the sky. "Is any of it?"

"No." He knelt, too, while Daniel and Poppy looked on, and gently placed his hand on the grass. Golden magic drifted from his fingers in slow motion, shining star pinpricks. The grass underneath flickered true green before fading into again. "See?"

I imitated Berron, placing my hand over the grass and allowing my borrowed Gentry magic to bathe the grass like rain. Green played over a few blades before disappearing, like a fire that wouldn't start.

Deep in my awareness, Patty Melt the fire mouse twitched, rolled over, and went back to sleep.

I stood, shook off the chill and the dreams of sleepy fire creatures. "Where to now?"

"Through the Forest of Emeralds." Berron turned away and started walking. His moth eyespots watched us follow.

We walked in silence, our footsteps muffled by the soft grass. No bird sounds or wind disturbed the still air. Nothing in sight justified the sparkling green name of this place. Certainly not the silent lightning that stole across the sky.

Then Daniel spoke. "Berron?"

"Daniel," he replied, without slowing or looking back.

"Where are we, exactly?"

I almost expected Berron to make a smart remark in response. Instead, he was like a graduate teaching assistant explaining a concept to a freshman class, suddenly the Berron I'd met that first day at the restaurant. "You're familiar with the concept of parallel universes, of course."

"Is this a reflection of our world, then?" Daniel asked. "Are we standing in Central Park right now?"

"Why does it always have to be a reflection of *your* world? Who said *you* were primary?" Berron stopped, and laid his hand with tenderness on a tree trunk. "If anything, your world is a pale reflection of *this*."

"But do they overlap? Are they linked?" Daniel continued, a little too intensely.

Poppy caught my eye and raised an eyebrow.

Berron, who missed nothing, calmly replied to Daniel: "Why do you ask?"

"Just curious, I guess."

Berron scoffed. "'Just curious'? 'I *guess*'? How many times in your life have you said those words?" He came a step closer to Daniel than would have been considered polite. "You want to know where you are? You're still stuck in Manhattan. The borders closed here when they closed outside. You're not getting out this way, Danny Boy."

Daniel looked like he wanted to lay Berron out on the cold grass.

Berron spun, setting his black-edged capes aflutter, and continued ahead without a backwards glance.

Poppy leaned close to me. "So it is the same. Only with different things in it. We could be standing in Central Park. Or in that gelato place on Columbus Circle."

"No gelato here, I'm afraid," Berron called back. He must have had exceptional hearing, or something about the silence carried whispers to his ears. "But we won't starve. Not immediately," he added, cheerfully.

Daniel rolled his eyes, the only comment that couldn't be overheard by the Prince.

I wanted to share Daniel's annoyance, share a private laugh, like we always had—but then I remembered who he'd been talking to, and the chuckle died on my lips.

11

With nothing to break up the scenery, no animal sounds to startle or enchant us, it seemed like the cold, dark woods stretched on and on. When there were greater spaces between the trees, and the boiling dark green clouds broke apart for a few moments, the sky revealed itself studded with faint crystal stars, like someone had cracked open an agate geode at midnight.

Was it day? Was it night? How would anyone know? Time slipped.

I could no longer be sure how long we'd been in the woods.

Then a structure rose before us, blotting out the clouds and sky and forest alike, with layers like a wedding cake, but tilted, as if the structure spiraled upward from the ground. Something that looked like barbed wire surrounded the base and seemed to line each layer of the structure itself.

Any of us could have spoken up as we approached. None of us did. The silence in that place cast its own kind of spell. It was only as we drew closer that the barbed wire turned itself into scraggly tree branches, on trees far shorter than the ones we'd left behind.

An orchard. Withered apples hung from the branches.

I stopped and reached for one of the apples.

"Ask first," Berron said. "Before you touch anything."

"I wasn't going to pick it—"

"It's okay." He came up to the tree I was standing next to and pulled a branch into reach. "They're edible. At least, they used to be."

I carefully touched an apple. The skin was dry and textured, like old velveteen. I remembered the wild apples I'd sliced and served to Daniel and Berron. Before—well, everything.

"They'd probably trap you here," Daniel said. "Like Persephone."

"I don't need to give people anything to make them want to stay with me," Berron replied coolly.

It was Daniel's turn to look like murder.

"No one's eating anything," I said. "We have bigger things to do." I pushed past Berron and led the way.

A natural path opened up between the two sides of the orchard, leading to the base of the looming structure. With a clear view, I could see that the base was crafted of great stones that somehow fitted together to form a wall. Carvings marked each boulder with unique swirls and patterns. Instead of mortar, grass sealed the spaces in between. And since every layer was smaller than the next, the roof made a spiral pathway up to the top of the structure, with apple trees like sentries on every level. "The Fortress of Apples," I said.

"Home," Berron replied.

A whinnying sound came from somewhere near the structure.

"Oh, good Lord," Poppy said. "A horse!"

A dappled horse with a shaggy mane peeked out from around the curve of the fortress. It was the same one Berron had ridden down the street on the day the restaurant opened to friends and family: dark gray with a spattering of white stars across its body, like a telescope picture of a faraway galaxy.

Poppy clapped her hands. "I *love* horses. Haven't ridden one in positively *ages*."

"Sybelia doesn't take to others very well," Berron said.

As if in agreement, the horse huffed, then whirled around and retreated behind the curve.

Poppy visibly deflated—but her hands twisted over themselves, as if she was restraining herself from running after the beautiful animal. I knew the feeling. Sometimes I simply *had* to pat Jester's cute little floppy ears, even if it annoyed the living daylights out of him.

"Why isn't the horse asleep?" asked Daniel.

"It's not entirely of this place. There used to be a lot more back and forth, long ago, before it became too dangerous, and the horses here mixed with those of the outside."

"But how do you feed it?" Poppy said. "If the food here isn't good."

"It's good enough for Sybelia to get by, but I bring more from outside when I visit."

"She can eat food from the human world?"

Berron nodded. "Just like me."

"Berron," I said, "what *about* you? Why aren't you asleep like everything else?"

Poppy and Daniel looked at him.

"I was chosen." He opened his hands, palms up, and gold magic drifted above them like dust motes. "To stay awake. Because I seemed the most resistant to sleep."

I realized what we *hadn't* seen on the walk through the Forest of Emeralds, or the approach to the Fortress of Apples.

The Gentry.

When Berron said they were all asleep, I'd pictured them like Sleeping Beauty—restfully curled up somewhere, but still *visible*. "Where is everyone else?"

"You want to see them?"

I nodded, slowly, not sure what I was agreeing to, exactly.

I expected him to open the Fortress or something, lead us in. Instead, he laid both hands on the nearest apple tree.

"Help me," he said.

"I don't know what to do—"

"You don't have to." The look on his face said this wasn't easy for him, not magically, not in any sense.

I shut up and put my hands on the tree.

"Think wakeful thoughts," he said.

Wakeful thoughts: Jester licking my face. The smell of Denver omelets and toasted bagels. Yellow sunbeams creeping across the four-poster bed. Car horns and emergency sirens. Just another day in the Big Apple.

What would it be like to wake up in the *Fortress* of Apples?

Our Gentry magic waltzed across the bark, then mingled together. When the golden magic combined, it was as if it suddenly became heavy, like flecks of gold in a miner's pan, and each stream of dust tumbled down the tree until it reached the top of the slightly exposed roots.

Beneath the roots, beneath the earth, I saw a glow. Then a face, half-hidden by a sheaf of golden hair. A hand pillowing the sleeping face. A rounded shoulder in a gold gown.

I gasped. And I could see, out of the corner of my eye, that Poppy's jaw had dropped, and Daniel's face was open with wonder.

"Not too much," Berron cautioned. "Don't want to startle her."

I decaffeinated my thoughts, as much as I could, while maintaining the flow.

The glowing being shifted, curling into the roots, scrunching her face up like a baby who wasn't ready to wake. She wasn't a baby, though. She looked sixteen. A sweet, golden sixteen in appearance, though perhaps older in human years.

"Do you see, now?" he asked.

I nodded. He withdrew his hands and I immediately withdrew mine as well. The sleeping apple girl disappeared from view under her blanket of roots and earth. I lifted my head, surveyed the grove. The Forest of Emeralds beyond. Imagined the miles of terrain around us. "All asleep?"

"Every one of them."

"And if you try to wake them?"

"It only works for a few seconds. I stopped trying." He shook his head. "At least you were all wearing natural fibers. I can't imagine being woken to the smell of rayon and polyester." He attempted to smile at his own joke.

Berron was going through some things. "Can we go to the top?" I said. "I want to see the lay of the land."

"I think I'll stay here," Poppy said, seizing Daniel's arm. "I want to run some tests."

"Is it safe?" I asked Berron.

"There's literally no one here, Zelda. Why wouldn't that be safe?"

I punched his shoulder, glad to have an outlet for the unease I was feeling. "Don't go too far," I said to Poppy. "Daniel, watch her back while she's working."

"Got it."

Poppy met my gaze, and with a single, small nod, showed me that she was carrying out the plan we'd made before we left. Daniel knew that Poppy read minds, but if he thought she was concentrating on something else, he might let down his guard long enough for a few stray thoughts to slip.

I needed to know what he was thinking.

I needed to know if I could trust him. Or not.

With the two of them wandering off into the grove, I followed Berron. The climb to the top took turn after turn around the spiral fortress. There still weren't any doors, only the flat boulders carved with symbols. The ground that made up the roof of each level appeared to be as solid as the ground below. Was there anything at all inside the Fortress, or was it only a monument?

We passed tree after tree until we reached the top circle, which was ringed by stones set into the edge like a low wall. Forest rolled out in every direction. Farther out, the trees dropped away to patches of open fields. A silent stream snaked through the distance, shimmering, leading to a shoreline of glassy, slate-colored water. And beyond that—

Only the lightning-covered clouds, thick and forbidding as walls.

I tried to overlay my mental map of Manhattan on this landscape, and failed. It was too big, too strange, too different to even begin to match up something as earthly as, say, the Empire State Building, with the land before me. Manhattan pulsed with life. This place lay silent, its people trapped.

Berron leaned on the stones, looking outward. His hair should have blown in some kind of cinematic, princely breeze, but it just hung around his face like a veil.

"You put up a good front with your jokes and your charm," I said.

He didn't reply.

I paused, taking in the view, feeling like I wouldn't stop seeing it even when I closed my eyes for sleep, safely back in my own room. "You're all alone. *Truly* alone. And yet you didn't dare let on how desperate you were. Why?"

He smirked. "Neediness isn't appealing."

"I would have been happy to help—"

"Would you?" he said mildly. "Or did you want to open your sandwich shop in peace?"

Touché. "Why not just kidnap me and drag me here? Command me to fix it? And don't tell me it's because you're not like that. I saw how you reacted when the restaurant was trashed."

Berron made a soft, amused noise. "You would have punched me in the face and run for it."

I considered. "Yeah, I would have." Then I had an unwelcome thought. "Unless you somehow compelled me..."

He threw his head back, smiled like he might weep. "I'm not a god. If I were, I would have fixed this. Of course I charmed you. I *had* to charm you. You were the last hope I had."

I grabbed his jacket, turned him to face me. "No. I am *not* your last hope. We are *all* your hope. Poppy. Daniel—"

He gave a derisive laugh, and shook his head.

"Shut up. Him too. And Victorine, and James, and Aunt Belinda, and—and even the dogs! Jester would *so* kiss your face right now."

That made him laugh. A short laugh, but enough to chase the despair from his face. "When I finally broke out of the Mirror," he said, "all I knew was that your grandmother was already gone. That her children, and her children's children, were far beyond my reach. I never thought you'd come back. I thought—" He paused, looked out across the Forest. "I thought we were doomed. Now you're here. You're really here…" He trailed off, took a great breath. "Even if nothing works—I tried—"

I gave him a little shake, which was a little like trying to shake an elm tree. "Don't say that. We haven't even started yet."

From far below, a cry of "Tally ho!" rose over the grove.

Berron and I leaned over the ring of stones and looked down.

Dashing down the center of the apple tree grove was Poppy, mounted bareback on Berron's supposedly unfriendly horse, Sybelia, whooping with triumph as her yellow and green cape whipped in the wind behind her.

Daniel was nowhere to be seen.

"Damn it," I said to myself. "She was supposed to be—"

"Supposed to be what?"

"Nothing."

"I don't believe you."

"I don't care."

Poppy expertly rode Sybelia around the side of the structure to where the roof met the ground, then took the grass-roofed spiral upwards.

Sybelia whinnied with horsey pride as Poppy brought her to a stop. "'Allo, guv'nor," Poppy said, tipping an imaginary hat.

"That's my horse," Berron pointed out.

"And a right proper one she is," Poppy said. "Sweet as clover and twice as clever." She leaned down and hugged the horse's neck. "Isn't that right, old girl?"

To see her astride Sybelia, in her Mustardseed costume, she looked like she'd ridden right out of a fairy forest.

Which, in fact, she had.

12

P oppy threw one leg over the horse and slid down, landing on the grass with a thump. She dug into her pockets and came up with two packets of McVitie's Digestive Biscuits. "'Doesn't take to others' doesn't apply when you have these," she said, handing the packets to Berron. "Mind the animal, my good sir, whilst I confer with my colleague."

Berron blinked at the cookies.

Sybelia shuffled forward and attempted to snarf the packages whole.

Poppy drew me away, down the spiral, away from Berron. "Something's fishy," she said quietly.

"How would you know? You've been having horsey time!"

"Rude." She looked over her shoulder to make sure we were alone. "I can see Daniel's thoughts just as well when I'm riding by on a horse. He lets down his guard and he might as well be holding up signs."

I didn't know whether to walk faster, to get more distance from Berron, or slow down, to avoid running into Daniel at the bottom of the Fortress.

Poppy saved me from choosing by threading her arm through mine as we continued, drawing me closer and matching my pace to hers. "He's looking"—she lowered her voice to a whisper—"for *vampire magic*."

I stopped short, nearly slingshotting Poppy off the side of the Fortress. "He *what*?"

"Don't *murder* me, I was just doing what you asked." She brushed off her costume, pushed her hair behind her ears, and took my arm again, only with me on the outside of the path this time.

"Sorry! Sorry," I said. It was my turn to glance back, make sure we weren't being overhead. "You mean he was thinking about... that magic?"

"Not just thinking. *Looking*. Actively searching Everything he sees, he's checking."

I felt an unaccustomed surge of gratitude for my brother, Bruce, who had introduced me to Poppy in the first place. Not only was she a fire witch and a mind-reader, but I could absolutely trust her, unlike the two fine-looking gents currently above and below me. "I mean, I was going to look for unusual magic here, but why would he be so intense about it? This is the Gentry's turf. There shouldn't *be* any of that here."

"I *know*." Her eyes widened with a thrill of horror and curiosity.

"*Is* there any?" My gaze darted around, as if I'd somehow missed a red glow on the wilted grass, or the withered apples, or the looming forest. I *could* see vampire magic, since I had topped up on it recently enough, but to my eye, there was none to be seen.

Then, another unwelcome thought: What if Daniel was better at seeing it?

We'd never tested it before. I had no way of knowing for sure. And to ask him questions would mean giving away that I knew something was up.

I could have growled in frustration.

"Don't look now, but here comes your Blessed ex-boyfriend," Poppy said. "And maybe try to look less like you might take his head off."

I managed a tight smile. I'd be lying if I said I wasn't already thinking of a dozen ways to sneak the truth out of him. Disguising myself as Jessica, for a start.

Daniel ran up the incline with his customary athleticism, augmented by his vampiric strength and stamina. He jogged to a stop before us and put his hands on his hips, breathing as if he'd been winded—but he wasn't winded.

He was performing being human.

"Where's the horse?" he said.

Poppy gestured upward, airily. "I left her with Berron."

Meanwhile I was calculating exactly how far away he was standing from Poppy, and how I could maneuver him close enough so she could keep reading him.

Daniel looked at me. "Do I have something in my teeth?"

"I was admiring your costume," I said, intentionally delivering the words evenly, neutrally. I wasn't concealing that something was wrong. I was communicating it. A warning shot, for an old game. A game we had played many times before. A game that blew up our relationship.

A game I liked to call *Who Breaks First?*

He shifted weight from foot to foot, once. A tell he hadn't learned to conceal. He knew something was off, and it made him uncomfortable. "I'm glad you like it," he said.

"Admiring isn't the same as liking."

A disbelieving laugh. "So you don't like it?"

"Maybe I miss your usual suits."

"Maybe you can get used to me in this one."

"I haven't made up my mind."

Poppy stepped forward and waved a hand between Daniel and me. "Hello? Perhaps we should be—I don't know, just theorizing here—investigating why this whole place has withered away? Perhaps you could discuss your sartorial opinions... *later?*"

"Absolutely," Daniel said. Eye contact so intense it almost hurt to hold it, like handfuls of ice.

Berron approached from behind us, with Sybelia in tow. "I host a party," he said, "and all my guests wander off."

It took a mile-deep sense of dark humor to be talking about parties. Still, it gave me an excuse to turn away from Daniel. "If this is a party, Berron, you need a better caterer."

"Are you volunteering?" His charm was back in full force.

"Maybe. What kind of kitchen you got?"

"Follow me, chef." Berron led the way back to the base of the Fortress. When we reached ground level, he walked around the structure, running one hand over the boulders as we went. Then he stopped in front of one emblazoned with triple spirals. "My kitchen," he said. "And everything else."

The boulder under his hand swung silently away, leaving an opening the approximate size and shape of a doorway in the side of the Fortress. From within, a warm light glowed—a welcome contrast to the slow death pressing down on us outside.

I stepped through the opening.

And gasped.

By the light of golden-flamed lamps, I saw the craftsmanship of the Mirror Seal a hundred times over, executed in extravagant furnishings and carved walls and polished wood floors so shiny they could have been mirrors themselves.

A great heap of pillows and rich velvet coverlets embroidered with metallic threads and studded with sparkling crystals filled one corner of the room. Dried flower petals and herbs had been crushed over the bedding, leaving behind a scent like Cleopatra's long-lost perfume.

Another corner held a stool, some pieces of wood, and carvings in progress, the fresh-cut shavings adding to the scent of the room. A third corner embraced a fireplace nook with a vent hood in the shape of an upside-down flower. Wooden cabinets with wavy glass fronts framed a built-in writing desk along one wall. It was like a ship's cabin, but lavish beyond dreams.

"Oh, my," murmured Poppy.

Daniel came in last, and said nothing, though his gaze traced everything in the room.

Berron went to the cabinets and began pulling out earthenware mugs. "I haven't had any visitors in a while…"

"Why *not*?" Poppy said. "If I had a place like this I'd practically be dragging people over to have a look." She scooped up a velvet coverlet and pressed it to her face, inhaling the scent.

"Yeah, nice place you got here, Berron," Daniel said. He leaned against the wall and crossed his arms.

I shot him a look, but he seemed sincere enough.

"Oh—chairs!" Berron dropped the mugs onto a countertop with a muffled clatter. "I forgot about chairs." He hurried outside.

Poppy ran over and peeked out. "He's putting his hand on another boulder. He's going in. And… he's bringing out chairs! How does *that* work?" She moved aside as Berron came back in.

"I don't have visitors much. Or—well—ever, anymore," Berron said, carefully setting down the chairs. He brought over the stool, too, and the chair from the writing desk. "But it's no trouble to call up a few extras."

"How did you do that?" I asked.

He had gone back to the fireplace, where he was making some kind of hot drink out of pinches of dried substances he plucked out of various jars. "The Fortress of Apples, as you may have guessed, is enchanted. We are not much on *things—*"

Daniel looked around the room and raised an eyebrow.

"But for those who prefer to be more sheltered, the Fortress can provide what is needed. This is my room, should I choose to be in residence."

"Like the queen," Poppy said, running her fingers over the writing table. "So if anyone else opened up one of those boulders, they'd find their own room?"

"Or whatever they require. Jousting lances. Glow-in-the-dark silk. Barrels of apple blossom honey. And when they're done with it, they load it back into the Fortress."

I chuckled and took a chair. "Easy cleanup," I said.

"Exactly."

Daniel hadn't moved. "Berron, do you have any theories on why your world is dying?"

Both Poppy and I turned to look at Daniel. Like—the man just invited you into his house, and he's making you tea? Maybe don't bludgeon him with the hard questions yet?

Daniel returned my gaze steadily. *I'm here for a reason*, it said, *and so are you.*

I shifted uncomfortably.

Berron handed me a steaming mug, with a hint of a smile to let me know he wasn't bothered. I returned the smile, grateful for the drink and his ability to be patient with Daniel's bluntness.

The second mug went to Poppy, who sniffed at it delightedly.

The third mug he carried to Daniel, who eyed it like it was hot dog water before taking it.

"I'm not trying to kill you," Berron said. "If I wanted to do that, I'd use one of the stakes I made specifically for the purpose." He glanced at the woodworking corner, where some of the pieces I'd originally taken for walking sticks turned out to have very sharp points, and the smaller sticks were the exact size of arrows.

"Good to know," Daniel replied.

"He is here to help, you know," I added, to Berron.

"Why, though?" Berron asked. "It's a fair question, isn't it? Why *are* you here, Daniel?"

I jumped in. "You know why. Because when the Mirror Seal was created, it was a treaty between the Gentry, the Blessed, and the witches. It only makes sense to have all three investigating what might have gone wrong to cause *this* to happen," I said, gesturing at the world in general.

"As much as I enjoy every syllable of your dulcet tones, my Zelda," Berron said, gently, "I didn't ask you. I asked your ex."

I had to restrain myself from throwing the mug and yelling *Don't call me your Zelda, and don't call him my ex*, but I wouldn't give Berron the satisfaction of watching me lose it. Instead, I slurped angrily at the hot liquid. Damn him, but it was tasty. I usually hated roses and lavender in anything, but this worked. Like a pack of cherubs had made their own version of Sleepytime tea.

Daniel took a long, slow sip from his mug. Then he casually crossed the room, set down the mug, and picked up one of the wooden stakes. He twirled it between his fingers, pressed the point against his palm. Observed the red indentation it left behind. "I don't know why none of you seem to trust me." He looked at Poppy. "You're reading my mind every time I get close enough."

She opened her mouth, as if to protest, then closed it as Daniel continued.

"I may not be able to feel when you're doing it, but the look on your face says you're trying as hard as you can, every chance you get. We hardly know each other."

Poppy's gaze dropped to her mug.

Daniel spun the stake again, pointed the sharp end at Berron. "And you—you act like we're old enemies. Like we ought to fight to the death. But other than help Zelda restore her restaurant, and maybe get turned into a vampire—"

"Blessed," I corrected, automatically.

"I haven't even *been* one long enough to remember to censor myself." He returned his attention to Berron. "I haven't done anything to you. Whatever your beef is with the Blessed, I'm not part of it."

Berron rolled his eyes and made a disbelieving noise.

Daniel flipped the stick around, pushed the dull end at the prince. "Take it. Go on. If you mistrust me so much, why not get me out of the way right now?" With his other hand, he pressed the sharp point under his sternum. "Go ahead."

Berron wrapped his hand around the base of the stake.

They locked eyes.

Poppy made as if to intervene, but I shook my head.

I wanted to see what they would do.

"Go ahead. Do it," Daniel said.

Berron slowly applied pressure until the point of the stake was clearly about to make a hole in Daniel's new shirt. "You'd like that, wouldn't you," he said. "Master of the universe, reduced to nothing by a change of circumstances."

"You call getting turned into *this* a 'change of circumstances'?" Daniel managed to say, as the pressure of the sharp point began to cut off how deeply he could breathe.

"Poor Daniel. All that wealth, all that power, trapped on a tiny island for the rest of his unnatural life. Forced to drink blood—or worse, be *brought* blood—to stay alive. Better to antagonize someone, get them to take away any choice you might have had about dealing with it. Better than being alone in a world that despises you, with friends who no longer trust you. Or no friends at all." Berron leaned in, harder. That point had to *hurt*. "Don't you think I know what it's like? To be alone? To be forced to beg for help? To wish I could lay it all down and give up? Of course I don't want you around. You remind me of everything I hate." He withdrew the stake suddenly, drawing it back like a javelin—and hurled it across the room, where it sank into the wall with a thunk and quivered. "But I'm not allowed to lie down and die. And neither are you." He retrieved Daniel's mug, and his own. "To fighting. For the right things."

Daniel stood, frozen, and for a moment I wasn't sure if he was finally going to take that swing at Berron. Or walk out.

Then, he chuckled. Shook his head. Took the mug and clanked it against Berron's. "You're something else, you know that?"

"So I've been told," Berron said.

They drank. They both laughed.

And Poppy and I traded relieved glances.

Only I knew the secret that Daniel still kept. If I let it steep, like the rose and lavender tea, would it be too bitter to drink in the end?

13

T hough we emerged from Berron's quarters sometime later, the light in the sky hadn't changed, and neither had the temperature. It was as if no time had passed at all. As the four of us climbed to the top of the Fortress again, I asked Berron why.

"It's always this way, now."

"No seasons?"

He shook his head.

"No... clocks?"

"There never were, exactly. They don't work right here. But we had mornings and afternoons and nights, if that's what you mean."

We kept climbing. Poppy looked over the edges for a glimpse of Sybelia. Daniel kept a steady pace, with his gaze fixed on the path as if watching for obstacles.

When we reached the top, I walked a circle, scanning the horizon and trying to put together the mental map I had failed to assemble the first time.

There was our world, and there was the Forest of Emeralds. And there was also the blasted ice field of the Arcade. They appeared

109

different at first—but what if they weren't? What if they were all related? Could they share points in common?

Like the layers of a cake. There was a gluten-free French bakery Lily frequented on the Upper East Side that made a mille crepe cake consisting of dozens of thin crepes piled one on top of the other, layered with vanilla pastry cream.

Or maybe it was more like layers of fabric sewn together in Lily's workshop. Each piece of fabric was distinct, but threads passed through each layer, creating points where the layers touched very closely.

The Mirror was west of the Fortress, just as the Mirror was west of Central Park in our own world. The Hudson River and the East River had their twins on either side of this island, too, although the far shores were walled off by storms. If the logic of this layout continued in every direction, then to the north would be the North Woods. The scent of starfruit came back as if it were under my nose at that very moment—and at the same time, something flashed faintly red in the distance.

I stared north, but it was gone. Had I imagined it? I slowly turned my head to the side, letting my peripheral vision have a crack at it.

There it was again. Almost nothing, almost an illusion, an aura, like the afterimage when you stare at a lightbulb too long. "Daniel," I said, without turning to look for him, lest I lose what I was barely seeing. "Come here."

He came to my side.

"Look out there." I pointed as best I could without looking directly at it. "Do you see it?"

"See what?"

"Just—look."

He looked into the distance. "There *is* something out there."

"Red, right?"

He nodded.

"I can't see it when I look straight at it," I said.

Daniel's brow furrowed as he concentrated. "I can. But it's really faint."

I squeezed my eyes shut, rubbed them, then opened them again. "Berron," I said, "is there a small field of white flowers to the north of here?" I pointed where I'd seen the red. "Right around there?"

He had been leaning casually against one of the trees, but he quickly pushed away from the trunk and came to the edge of the roof. "How did you know that?"

"I've been there."

"You can't have been there—"

I shook my head. "Not here. In our world. My world." A feeling rose in my body, not unlike the instinct that something in the oven was in the process of browning. Kitchen alchemy. An awareness earned from a lifetime in kitchens, witness to the changing states of bread and meat and vegetables. Grandma always told me I'd develop that sense. I'd just never imagined it would apply to magic. "I think one of the Blessed has been there," I said. "Here. In the Forest of Emeralds."

Berron and Poppy immediately looked at Daniel.

Daniel raised his hands. "It wasn't me. I've never been here before."

"No one said you had," I said. "But we need a closer look. Now."

Poppy peered north. "That's quite a long way." She dusted her hands. "I'll just have to ride the horse."

"Any objections, Gentry prince?" I asked Berron.

"Anything my lady wishes," he murmured.

I smiled to myself as I looked out over the black-and-white landscape one more time. *Finally.* A break. A clue. Something was cooking. "Down we go," I said. "To the ground—and Sybelia."

Poppy clapped.

When we reached the ground, we found Sybelia browsing the fallen apples. I had never seen someone mount a horse bareback, only by stepping into a stirrup, but Poppy gripped part of Sybelia's mane, did a little hop-skip that swung her leg up, and she flew onto the horse's back almost like magic.

Daniel, Berron, and I walked alongside. We had our magical stamina to keep us going, whereas Poppy did not, but Sybelia would close the gap.

Standing together, facing north—it felt like we were a team. Maybe Berron and Daniel had to fight it out to clear the air. Or maybe it was the funny outfits, that now seemed right, somehow, like we never could have worn anything else. Or perhaps it was nothing more complicated than the way we flanked Poppy, gracefully astride Sybelia, and walked into the unknown.

We belonged to each other, now. And to this land.

I shook my head. I was getting weirdly poetic. Must have been the tea affecting my brain. Berron had probably put something in it. I tugged one of his capes until he leaned close, then I whispered in his ear. "Did you put anything funny in the tea?"

"I didn't think you'd be so quick to whisper sweet nothings in my ear, my dear Zelda. And although I'm enjoying it—what *are* you talking about?"

I rolled my eyes and pushed him away. "Never mind, you jackass."

With a self-satisfied smirk, he tipped his head back and ran his fingers through his hair.

Sybelia's hooves hit the turf with soft thuds, and Poppy swayed in rhythm. I put my hand on the horse's flank, occasionally, as we walked. The cold air made me long for Poppy's townhouse, and Jester curled up by my feet, his sandpapery toe beans pressed into my bare soles, upturned by sitting sidesaddle on the couch.

I rubbed my arms. "Is it getting colder?"

Berron looked concerned. "You aren't getting sleepy, are you?"

"No..." At least I didn't *think* I was. I didn't like the sound of that question at all.

"Perhaps I should warm you."

Daniel cut him off. "Let's run for a while," he said.

I looked at Daniel—who was, in fact, completely serious. "You want to *run*."

He shrugged. "It'll warm you. You have the energy for it." He held his hand out, like an offering. "Or I can top you up if you need it."

"I could use fire magic to warm you," Poppy said, "but it's temporary."

Berron slid into the lead, bringing Sybelia to a stop with a fond pat, and watched us with his dark eyes.

I reached up to Poppy and took her hand. "I'll take the fire magic." Daniel looked faintly disappointed as Poppy's fire magic swirled over me, warming me like a toaster element. "Much better," I declared.

Berron jogged backward, looking one-hundred-percent mischievous. "Pity," he said. "I'd wanted to go for a quick run." Then he spun, making his greatcoat capes flutter. "I guess I'll just have to make you all chase me." And with that, he tore off at a flat-out run.

"Oh, it's *on*." Daniel launched after him.

"Are you *serious*?" I said. But they were too far off, and all I heard was male laughter. "Men," I said.

Sybelia blew out a horsey breath, and it sounded like a Bronx cheer.

"Come on, old girl," Poppy said, patting my shoulder instead of the horse's. "Let's show them how it's done."

"Tally-ho!" I shouted.

And I ran. I ran like I was seven years old and didn't know the meaning of age, or tiredness, or pain. Poppy kept pace on Sybelia, whooping like an Amazon, as we plunged through the forest after Daniel and Berron.

Tree trunks whipped by. Branches reached for us but couldn't catch us, caressing us with the tips of their leaves as we dodged and ducked. I could almost imagine beings peeking around the great trees, watching with wide eyes as we thundered by.

The trees opened ahead. There was a field, and a long, narrow line cut into the earth, and exposed banks on either side forming a V in the land. At the bottom of the V, a thin, sparkling snake. My Florida brain took an extra half-second to register it for what it was.

A stream. A tiny, rushing stream.

The back of Daniel's jacket flipped upward as he leaped across, flashing the red lining before landing. He ran after Berron and disappeared into the forest on the other side of the stream.

Poppy urged Sybelia on, outpacing me as she prepared to make the jump. A rapid thunder of hoofbeats, then silence as Sybelia soared over the stream, suspended in midair, before shaking the ground with her landing on the far bank.

Old Zelda wouldn't have run full out after them. Old Zelda would have stopped and stepped carefully across.

Old Zelda had been left behind the day she caught a vampire wielding an unusually sharp cake knife.

I sprinted faster and launched myself after them, flying over the sparkling water winking at me like it had woken from its sleep just to cheer me on. I didn't even break stride when I hit the other bank—I just kept running like I'd never have to stop, my lungs miraculously breathing the cold air as easily as they would have on a gentle walk.

And there, tickling my nose once again, was the delicate aroma of freshly cut starfruit. Another clearing rolled out before me like an old shag carpet. Halfway across it, Daniel and Berron ran side by side.

Poppy charged ahead and nudged Sybelia between them. Daniel and Berron veered aside.

The path was clear. I put on a burst of speed and passed them both before drawing alongside Poppy and Sybelia for the final stretch.

And there, just ahead, was a small field of white flowers at the same time.

My momentum nearly carried me into them. I stumbled to a stop, just in time, to avoid trampling the plants. Poppy and Sybelia pulled up sharply, carving divots into the earth before the flowers began.

Daniel and Berron walked up, not winded in the slightest. "Good run," Daniel said, following my gaze to the flowers. "Warmer now?"

I nodded. Then I knelt, to get closer to the familiar, fruit-scented blossoms. Unlike the rest of the plants, the white flowers were dewy with life—

And glazed with red magic.

14

Poppy, Daniel, and I got on our hands and knees to examine the flowers as closely as possible. Berron, meanwhile, paced like an expectant father on his third espresso. "What do you see? Who did this? And how did they get in?"

"Settle down," I said. "No rushing. And *no magic*," I added quickly, to Poppy, who had raised her hand over the flowers like she was about to cast a spell. "Don't bleed on anything, either, Daniel."

Daniel shot me a look. "I don't normally drip blood."

"Just—don't. In our world, magic sends you through to where the Arcade is. Poppy's magic or your blood could trigger it. We're not ready for that."

"Why not?" Berron said. "Some *bloodsucker* clearly was. No offense, Daniel."

Daniel didn't respond, other than to poke a flower and squint at it.

I sat back on the grass, at the edge of the flowers. The smell of starfruit reminded me that I hadn't eaten anything in a while, if you didn't count Berron's tea. Maybe Sybelia would share some cookies.

I ran my hand over the grass, then brushed the soft white flowers themselves. "The magic could just be a residue of Victorine traveling to the Arcade from Central Park. Or me, even."

"But why would that bleed through here?" Poppy asked.

"If everything is connected," I said, "then maybe things leak."

Sybelia shuffled forward and took deep horsey sniffs at the flowers.

"Berron, get Sybelia," I said. "I can't be responsible for dimension-traveling horses."

Berron fished the squashed cookie packages from his pockets and lured Sybelia a safe distance away.

Poppy sat next to me on the grass, the tips of our shoes almost touching the flowers, as Daniel continued to examine the field. "What if we went through here?" Poppy asked. "Would we end up at the Arcade?" She paused, seeming to have a sudden thought. "Could we travel all the way through to Central Park?"

"Berron?" I called.

He approached, removed his coat, and spread it on the ground. "Here, sit on this." Poppy and I moved over with expressions of thanks. "The only way into the Forest of Emeralds should be the Mirror," he said, taking a seat on the grass next to us.

"How did you go back and forth before the Mirror?" I asked.

"There were places we could just... slip through. But they all closed."

I imagined doors shutting, one after another. "Weren't you worried about getting trapped in here?"

"No more than you worry about getting trapped in your world. The Forest of Emeralds is home. Why would I worry about getting trapped?"

"True," I said. "But… no one thought about what would happen if the Forest of Emeralds"—I hesitated, not wanting to sound insensitive—"failed?"

A sound of dark amusement escaped him. "You can't turn on the news without being reminded of how you're slowly burning the Earth to ash, yet you go about your business." He shook his head. "No one ever really believes the world will end."

"Jolly," Poppy said, throwing a piece of grass at him.

"The Mirror was supposed to be a stable way to cross through," I said, getting the conversation back on track. "Until it was closed by mutual agreement."

"An agreement so we didn't bring an end to those like our friend here." Berron nodded to Daniel, who gave a short, distracted wave before turning his attention back to the flowers.

"Why *do* you hate each other so much?" Poppy asked. "The Blessed and the Gentry, I mean. Not you and him specifically."

"You don't know?" Berron said.

Poppy shook her head. "No one talks about these things. Oh, witches are supposed to be all one happy family, but everyone's keeping their little secrets." She wiggled her fingers in a woo-woo motion.

"Do you know?" Berron asked Daniel.

Daniel shook his head. "Too new at this."

Berron nodded, and appeared to be thinking about how to respond. "The Blessed," he said, after a few moments, "view everything as a zero-sum game."

I blinked, trying to process this information. "As in... only one player can win?"

"They spend years jockeying for position. Gaining wealth. Becoming royalty in their own little domains. Anything that threatens that, well..." Berron drew his finger across his neck. "There were turf wars. We could have fought. But we had our own home to retreat to. And with the Peace in place, it made sense to stay there. Many of my people are shy by nature. Homebodies, if you will. But there were always those who were more adventurous."

"Heedless, you mean?" Poppy said.

"Heedless," Berron admitted. "For the sake of adventure." He was staring into the distance, as if remembering something.

A little more than six feet away, Daniel eased himself down into the flowers, then rolled onto his back. He put both hands behind his head and gazed up at the greenish storm clouds laced with gold lightning. He closed his eyes like this was any ordinary field, on any ordinary day.

"Daniel," Poppy said, "perhaps you shouldn't take a nap in the magic flowers?"

I watched him.

He lay there silently for what felt like a minute or so. Then, as if he sensed me watching, he opened his eyes. He turned and propped his head up, meeting my gaze. A private smile crossed his face, bringing me a flash of moments when he had done the same thing long ago—lazily, after rolling over in bed. Those eyes, those dark irises like black coffee backed by hellfire.

Then one hand went to his mouth like he had something in his teeth.

Teeth...

Not exactly polite, but who was I to judge? Still—

Why did it set off alarm bells in my brain?

He was nicking his finger.

"Daniel, no!"

He calmly smeared the bleeding fingertip against the white flowers.

Red marred the petals. His body, richly clothed in that black suit cobwebbed with white, framed by the crimson lining of his jacket, began to fade from sight with pinpricks of light so bright they left starry afterimages. "See you on the other side," he said.

He'd left his words left behind.

He was gone.

I scrambled to my feet and let out a streak of curse words that would have blasted the forest dead if it wasn't already. "Daniel!" I yelled at the flowers, uselessly, before lowering my voice. "I'm not your keeper," I added.

Even as it left my lips, I knew it wasn't true. I signed up to be his keeper. I practically signed in blood. I made him what he was. Didn't matter that he was my ex. Didn't matter that conversion had driven him into desperation. If I could have washed my hands and walked away, I wouldn't. I still—

I still *cared*. And it twisted my insides until I could have been sick on the flowers. How could I be soft enough to have let this flirtation, this nothing, slide past my defenses like a knife tipped with poisoned honey? This is how *other* people were supposed to feel. Not me. I could drink affection and seduction all day and never get drunk.

Couldn't I?

Daniel was a flirtation. And yet the whole world had narrowed to a Daniel-shaped space of crushed flowers.

The smear of his blood was gone as if the flowers drank it. Where he had gone through glowed brighter, redder, as if it had been refreshed and recharged with magic. It was the most vivid color in the forest, aside from our costumes.

"I told him he wasn't allowed to lie down and die," Berron said. "Why did he think he was allowed to lie down and disappear?"

"He's testing my theory," Poppy said.

Berron and I looked at her.

"Don't you remember? When we first sat down? I asked if this place crossed all the way over to Central Park."

I pressed my hand to my forehead. "Oh, Daniel. Daniel, you arrogant, reckless, swaggering *idiot*."

Berron looked impressed despite himself. "He's playing with his life."

"Don't encourage him!" I snapped.

"He's not even here," Berron said.

"Don't trouble me with details." I stretched my neck like I was about to dive into a pile of orders during the breakfast rush. "We have to go after him."

"Yes, but how?" Poppy said. "Through here? Or back to Central Park?"

I gestured to the flowers. "We're already here—"

Poppy shook her head. "But we don't know that this is a safe way. It *might* be a faster way to get to Daniel. Or it might be a dead end. Or worse."

I couldn't stop seeing Daniel with the Arcade. Shivering but determined. Bathed in the strange light of her glowing eyes. What deal would he make, if he could?

And what would he trade away in exchange?

He's playing with his life, Berron had said. But Daniel's wasn't the only life in play. Berron's people, the sleepers in the Forest of Emeralds. Poppy. Berron himself. I couldn't drag them through an untested portal to another world. "You're right," I said. "We can't risk it." I retrieved Berron's jacket from the ground, tossed it to him.

"Back to the Mirror?" he said.

I nodded decisively. "Back to Central Park."

Poppy was already bringing Sybelia over. She repeated the hop-skip-jump that landed her on Sybelia's back. Then she patted the horse's neck and murmured something that sounded reassuring.

I gestured at the horse. "How do I get on this thing?"

"You don't want to run?" Berron asked.

"I don't want to push it."

"Allow me." He held his hands to offer me a step up.

I hesitated only a fraction of a second before taking the help. I settled into position behind Poppy, grateful for the long pants that protected my legs.

"Hold on tight," Poppy said. "Without stirrups, it's much harder to stay on. Tighten your core and grip with your thighs."

"Horse Pilates," I muttered, wrapping my arms around her waist. "They'd charge a fortune for it if they could figure out how to copy it in an Upper East Side studio." Leave it to Berron to play the gallant gentleman assisting his lady. He made it easy to fall into.

Like a trap.

15

When we arrived back at the Mirror, I managed to get down from Sybelia myself, mostly by falling off. Poppy dismounted with a graceful slide. Berron patted the horse's neck, whispered something in her ear, and Sybelia took off in the direction of the Fortress, leaving the three of us alone.

The trees of the Forest of Emeralds towered over us, yet their branches drooped as if exhausted.

I sympathized. No matter how much energy I gained from magic, watching Daniel disappear through the field of flowers had taken it out of me. We had gone in as a matched set of four: Peaseblossom, Cobweb, Moth, and Mustardseed. We were going out as three.

Our set was broken. Was it wrong to take it personally?

Wherever Daniel had ended up, I had to find him. It was the only way I would get to yell at him until he promised to never do anything that stupid again.

The Mirror reflected everything distorted, from my dark hair streaked with gray, to my purple outfit, to my Doc Martens. "I'll go first," I said. We made a chain by holding hands; first me, then Poppy, then Berron.

I stepped through the wavy silver glass—

And fell.

I barely had time to cry out before I landed on a stone floor. I turned my head just in time to see Poppy falling through the Mirror behind me. I scrambled. "Watch out for Berron," I called. The floor was cold, so cold. I pressed my hands against the stone and pushed myself up.

This *was* the room in the New-York Historical Society, the museum where we'd come through the Mirror in the first place.

Wasn't it?

Except...

The room was black and white. *Everything* was black and white. The Mirror, black and white. All color drained. The room had been plain before, save for the Mirror, but it was plain beige and cream and brown, not this. In contrast to our surroundings, Poppy and I were a riot of color.

Poppy stood up slowly and brushed herself off. She turned, taking in the view of the entire room. "Has anyone else's vision turned into a black-and-white movie? Grayscale? Whatever you call it?"

Berron got to his feet and took a startled step backwards. "What in the world—"

"Don't say that," I interrupted, getting up. "Say, 'Zelda, I know exactly what's going on.'"

"I sure as hell don't," he said.

I went to the door that opened into the New-York Historical Society hallway, threw it open.

The hallway was silent. Also colorless.

I ran to the end of the hallway, toward the public area. Found an entrance to the exhibit halls. Slammed into the push bar so hard the door ricocheted off the wall. I had to hold up a hand to stop it from rebounding on me.

Not a single person in sight. Only Tiffany lamps, the famous exhibit hall filled with them. I'd been there before, more than once, to be hypnotized by their glowing rainbow colors. Stained glass flowers and fruit and dragonflies in every jeweled tone. They stood where they always had, except they weren't rainbow-colored anymore. The vivid glass was every shade of gray—and that's when I realized the second thing wrong.

They weren't lit.

Nothing was on. No lights. The illumination was coming from everywhere and nowhere, cold and whitish, like it was being filtered through a cloud.

It took a moment of standing there to realize the last thing bothering me.

There was no stink. Not even a background hint of it.

New York *smells*. Exhaust, river water, the Papaya King on the next block, the sweat of a million people crawling through concrete canyons. It's not pretty. It's a growling, belching, breathing thing that rolls and clings and follows you. But when it's not there—

You notice.

"Zelda!" Berron called.

I turned. The door swung closed behind me with a noise like a slammed refrigerator. I stalked down the hallway to where Berron had stuck his head out of the room with the Mirror. "What is this?" I said. "Where are we? Why is there no color? Why is there light everywhere even though the lights don't work?" I was breathing hard. I tried to slow down. "You travel between worlds like you're commuting on the subway. You're supposed to know these things."

He shook his head.

I made an exasperated noise. "This isn't where we came from. Something's wrong. And where's Daniel?"

"We'll find him—"

"Don't comfort me." I pushed past him. "We're going back through."

"No, we're not." Maddeningly calm.

Something about the way he said it made me pause. My hands balled into fists, tightened until I could feel the crescent of each nail in my palms. "Why?"

"Because there's something wrong with the Mirror," he said.

Of course there was.

Poppy was already peering at it up close. "Look," she said.

I looked.

Where I had been able to see my reflection before, now I couldn't. What had happened to the glass? I moved closer. Why did it look like the frozen surface of an ocean? I held out my hand, almost close enough to touch the glass, but not quite.

Cold.

The surface of the Mirror was covered with a thick layer of ice. Like it had been laid down with a very specialized Zamboni machine.

"Poppy, can you melt it?"

Poppy shook her head. "I can't," she said. "My magic won't work. I can't see your thoughts anymore, either." She lifted her hand in a movement I'd seen many times, the one where she conjured a flame on her palm.

Nothing happened.

I shot Berron a look. "We better not be trapped here. I owe Jester his special nighttime snuggle and snack." I tried to say it lightly. I don't think it worked.

I looked around for a chair or a stanchion. "I'm going to smash it."

"No!" Berron said. "If you break it, we could *really* be stuck."

Stuck. He wasn't kidding. Poppy looked grave, too, and somehow that was worse.

I faced the iced Mirror again. Wrapped my arms around myself and shivered. It's all fun and games until you're trapped in another world with no food and you can't get home to your miniature poodle. What I wouldn't have done to be in a warm kitchen, standing over a stove, turning hamburgers.

With that thought, the small, slumbering fire mouse rolled over in my mind, sharing a dream of hot griddles and flames. "Patty Melt," I whispered.

"Pardon?" said Berron.

I waved him to silence with the feeling that I held an ember, oh-so-delicate, that might be blown out by the wrong word, the wrong thought. Wherever my mysterious little mouse hid, she hadn't been snuffed out by the dampening effect this place had on magic. I laid my hands carefully on the Mirror frame before sliding them onto the ice.

"Help me," I said to Poppy and Berron. "I think I can melt it."

"How?" Berron said. He moved closer, and the warmth helped relieve the chill from the ice.

"Fire magic doesn't work here…" Poppy began. Then her face lit up. "Except yours works differently, doesn't it? You just need more power," she finished, laying her hand on my left shoulder as if she had read my mind, which she couldn't. She just knew.

Berron's face looked skeptical, but his hand curled over my right shoulder. I felt every fingertip.

Maybe their magic couldn't emerge here. There was no trace of it, visually. But it still existed—they carried it within. I knew that as instinctively as I felt the fire mouse's presence. So I opened myself to the magic again, let it work its way from their grip into my muscles like a deep-tissue massage. Poppy's magic, all silver fire; Berron's, green and gold vines.

Together their magics twisted into a green and gold vine with leaves of silver flame. It grew through me and began to spiral up my neck.

It tickled.

A tiny laugh escaped before I could stop it.

"Are you *giggling*?" Berron asked.

"Shut up. I don't giggle."

Poppy snorted. "She does, though."

"Thanks a lot, Poppy," I said.

"Friends to the end!" she chirped.

I held my hands over the iced Mirror. The numbing cold sharpened. I brought my palms together, cupped them, prayer-like, the outer edges of my hands pressed directly against the ice while my palms created a little igloo.

I let the vine reach into my mind. Poke the sleeping fire mouse.

Patty's whiskers twitched. She opened glowing ball bearing eyes. Her tail flicked back and forth. Then she delicately seized one of the fire leaves—

And stuffed it in her mouth.

She *ate* it.

Her cheeks bulged. She ate another. And another.

Following the vine.

All of this was going on in my head, as real as Jester's floppy ears, as real as Berron and Poppy's hands on my shoulders. Now all I had to do was guide the greedy little gal to the ice.

So I guided the magic vine into my fingers.

Patty Melt followed, curious and still hungry, nibbling more leaves on the way, tracing a path of intense heat down my left arm and wrist. Slowly, a glow rose from my cupped hands like a flashlight was pressed against my palms, shining through skin with an orange-pink radiance.

I pictured the vine growing in circles in my cupped hand, an all-you-can-eat magic buffet for a fire mouse with the munchies.

Some of us are conduits. We don't always choose it. My grandmother had been one. I'd fought or ignored it all my life until coming to Manhattan. Now I opened myself up to channel it all. To find Daniel. To get us out of here, wherever *here* was. To use a skill for the sake of others is the highest calling, whether that skill is building the West Side's greatest sandwiches or bringing the magic of fire and fae into your soul and making something new out of it.

This one's for you, Grandma.

A single drop of water gathered and rolled from beneath my hands.

Drip.

Then another. *Drip.*

And finally it began to stream down in little rivulets, pattering against the toes of my Doc Martens.

"The Mirror weeps," Berron said, with relief. He rested his head on top of the hand on my shoulder. Locks of his hair tumbled against my own.

Poppy added her free hand bracingly to my bicep.

It was hard to tell who was holding up whom. Poppy's solid grip didn't bother me. Berron's could have been distracting, to the point where I might have shaken him off in other circumstances.

I didn't.

Water dripped faster. I felt it on the toes of my boots, a steady spring melt. I heard a faint *plink* under my hands.

"It's cracking," Poppy whispered. "Keep going."

Berron took a deep breath, in and out, his head heavy.

A fresh surge of magic took me then. Heat rose through me along with something I could think of only as greenness—rising sap, flowing life itself. Spring thaw.

I channeled all of it to my tiny, radiant friend.

The musical plinks, *drip drip drip*, became an off-rhythm xylophone. The drips became a stream. A flood. I had to shift my hands almost to the edge of the Mirror to keep from falling through.

And then, the true surface of the Mirror was revealed again.

I released a breath with an almost disbelieving laugh. Berron and Poppy did the same.

"You did it!" Poppy said. "Well done, you."

"Well done, us," I said, clapping them both on the back. "Now let's get out of here before anything else happens."

"Agreed," Berron said, landing a brief kiss on my cheek. "Lead on, my Zelda."

And for once, I didn't correct him.

I just grabbed his hand and Poppy's, and took us through.

16

Colors returned. That was about the only good thing I could say about where we landed. We could have been anywhere else: the Forest of Emeralds; the New-York Historical Society; even the bleak ice field of the Arcade.

But no.

We had landed in a Victorian time capsule of couches, delicate side tables, lace, and antique knick-knacks. Warm, thick air. Cozy bordering on stuffy. Next to the couch, a porcelain stand with an assortment of walking canes. Satiny old wallpaper around a picture window. A wingback chair faced the window. Outside, tree canopies rose like balloons from a locked garden.

I knew this place. I knew that garden. The tasteful Oriental rug beneath my feet was the one that had cushioned Daniel's limp body as I sank my newly-grown canines into his neck.

A metallic taste flooded my mouth. Memory—or fear.

"Prospero," I said.

Poppy and Berron flanked me, Poppy to my left and Berron to my right. I didn't need to tell them where we were. Poppy had seen it in my thoughts before, and Berron had heard enough of the story to instantly recognize Prospero's home.

"Oh, my," Poppy said, surveying the room. She shifted her weight and opened both hands. Flames burst into life in her palms.

Berron seized a cane from the stand and pulled the handle away from the shaft, revealing a sword within. He smiled to himself, discarded the shaft, and took a second cane, removing the sword and throwing the second shaft aside. He whipped the two blades through the air. "Let's find out how 'Blessed' they really are."

"Stop waving those things around before you stab someone," I said.

"Stabbing someone is entirely the point."

"A pun! Oh, I *love* a pun," Poppy said. She nudged me. "'The point'? Get it?"

I would die for these people, if I didn't kill them first. "We should go," I said. "Before Prospero and friends show up."

"I'm not leaving the Mirror," Berron said.

The Mirror stood directly behind us, looking right at home in Prospero's living room, almost as if it had never been anywhere else. Seeing it here was like opening a kitchen cabinet and finding a gerbil circus inside. "The Mirror was hanging in the *museum*," I said. "I mean—it was *just there*. How can it be *here*?"

"They stole it, obviously," Poppy said. "While we were inside."

"How did they know to steal it then?"

"There are plenty of normals who work there," Berron said. "Any one of them could have been paid to tip off the Blessed."

I considered that. Pushed it aside, because we had bigger issues. "If the Mirror is here," I said, slowly, "and *we're* here... where's *Daniel?*"

The three of us looked at each other.

Poppy's eyes widened. "Did they... *do* something to the Mirror?" The flames in her hands flickered like dying candles before surging back to life.

Berron's expression turned grim. "Hold these," he said, handing me the swords. He went straight to the Mirror and felt around the edges, as if to see how it was hung. It wasn't hung at all. It only leaned against the wall. He pulled it forward, looked behind it. "I can't tell. But it's certainly suspicious the Mirror didn't lead to where it's supposed to go, right after we entered it."

"Right after they stole it," I said.

"What should we do now?" Poppy asked.

"We," Berron said, carefully tipping the Mirror down onto its long edge, "are going to steal it back."

"You're not serious," I said.

"Got any better ideas?" he said, easing it all the way to the floor, where it lay horizontal, on its side, propped against the wall. Ready to be carried away.

I looked at Poppy, who shrugged. "I don't think the Mirror will fit in the elevator," I said. "It's tiny."

"Then we'll carry it down the stairs." He removed a lace tablecloth from a table and draped it over the Mirror.

"Oh, great camouflage," I said.

"Grab the other end."

"I would, your Princeliness, except for these cocktail skewers." I lifted the swords and waved them.

"I'll hold them." Poppy extinguished her flames and relieved me. "Hey, how do pirates know they're pirates? Eh?" She brandished the swords. "They think—therefore they *arrr*!"

I put my face in my hands, briefly, before letting out a breath and picking up my end of the Mirror. "Whatever's going on, we'll figure it out later. We have to get this out of here and go rescue Daniel." *Or kill him for making me worry*, I didn't add.

Suddenly, there was a small sound.

I froze. The Mirror wasn't light, but my enhanced strength was enough to hold it under one arm while using my free hand to put my finger to my lips, gesturing Poppy and Berron to silence.

I had thought we were alone. Until I heard that involuntary *gasp*. Like the tiniest fizz of carbonation leaving a bottle of soda.

At Daniel's name.

I gave the room another look. Everything was in order, still the same overstuffed Victorian candy box, the fussy knick-knacks and the wildly outdated wallpaper, the overall effect a residence just this side of haunted house territory.

Except—

There *was* something.

Above the wingback chair, the one facing the window overlooking Gramercy Park, a faint crimson halo. So faint it could have been sunlight refracted by the antique window panes.

"Hang on," I said, trying to sound casual. "My boot's untied." I gestured for Berron to set the Mirror down. When we had it propped against the wall again, Poppy silently passed him the swords and relit her magical flames.

She'd read my mind. But Berron hadn't, so all I could do was point to the far chair and make vampire fangs with my fingers.

He looked confused at first, then understanding washed over his face. He nodded and took a better grip on the swords.

I crept closer to the chair back. Poppy and Berron fanned to the sides. I raised one Doc Marten-booted foot, and with a shout, I slammed it into the top of the chair, flipping the whole thing forward and dumping its occupant onto the floor directly below the window.

I rushed forward, a cry of "Don't move!" on my lips—which died away unsaid when I saw the curled up heap on the floor.

Jessica. Jessica, the arrogant vamp who'd taken Daniel to the brink of death. The one who'd met him in that Puerto Rican restaurant. Who left her French fries behind, unknowingly, for me. That Jessica wrapped her thin arms around herself and said, in dramatic tones, "Go ahead. Kill me."

I blinked. This wasn't what I remembered from before, when she rushed James at the New-York Historical Society like a rage-filled vampire valkyrie.

Berron gestured with the sword. "Get up and die on your feet."

"No killing, Berron! What did I tell you?"

"They kill people, Zelda! This one nearly killed your ex-boyfriend!" He scoffed. "What did you expect? She'd make us a nice cup of *tea*?"

Jessica's deeply shadowed gaze shifted from Berron to me.

"I didn't ask for your opinion," I said to Berron. I was still trying to line up this version of Jessica with the one I'd seen before. The near-killer. The berserker. Curled up on the floor unwilling to fight.

Poppy moved a little closer.

"Careful," I said.

"I can handle it," Poppy replied. Her gaze moved over Jessica, slightly out of focus as if looking just beyond her shoulder. "She's afraid," Poppy said.

"Yeah, I'd be afraid too, if some hulking dude was waving *swords* at me," I said, with a pointed look at Berron.

"No—I mean, *yes*—but that's not it. She's afraid of... what is that?" She looked directly at Jessica and made a confused face. "Wrinkles?"

"*Wrinkles?*" I echoed.

"Stop looking at my mind, witch," Jessica snapped. Still insolent. At least something was familiar.

But I didn't have time for this. We needed to get the Mirror away. We needed to get to Daniel. And every minute we stood around here talking about the weather was another minute for Prospero and whoever else to return. "Get up," I said. "You're coming with us."

Jessica buried her face in her arms and groaned. "Why? Just leave me here and let me die."

"You heard her," muttered Berron.

"Shut up," I said. "I have an idea. Berron and I will carry the Mirror. Poppy, you bring Little Miss Goth. If she acts up, flame her like a creme brulee."

"On it," Poppy said. "Come along, missy. Up you get."

Jessica got to her feet with an exaggerated eye roll and an even bigger sigh. "We're all going to die."

"Everything dies," I said. "But not today. Now march. Wait," I added. "Where's Prospero? How long have we got?"

Jessica shrugged.

"I think we should just go," Poppy said. She prodded Jessica into the lead.

Berron and I balanced the great Mirror between us. It wasn't hard to carry, exactly—not with my borrowed strength—but damned if it wasn't incredibly unwieldy, and very easy to smack into walls. "Open the door," I said.

Jessica paused for a moment, probably just to show she could, then opened it.

We made our way into the dim hallway, lit with faded yellow light from ancient sconces. The cooler air woke me up like a wet washcloth to the face.

"Go, go, go," I said to Poppy.

Poppy aimed her palms at Jessica and made a shooing motion.

Jessica dragged her feet down the hallway.

Berron smirked. "I told you I should have—"

"No." I hefted the Mirror into a better hold and kept moving.

We reached the tiny elevator at last. I eyeballed the door. Thanks to years of stocking walk-in refrigerators and dry-goods pantries, I was a pretty good judge of size. Tilt the Mirror down, turn it on its side, take it in to the left before half-straightening it up, and it would just fit. In a horrible, claustrophobic way. With maybe one person. Two, if the second person could squish. You'd need two to maneuver it out again. Otherwise you'd just be stuck at the bottom, holding up the elevator while you waited for your partner to run down the stairs.

Except two in the elevator meant only one left to guard Jessica. And ride down alone with her. Since I needed Berron's extra strength to lift the Mirror, Poppy would have to be the guard.

Poppy caught me looking at her. "What?" Her gaze drifted over my shoulder. "You think I can't take her? Rude." She tossed her hair back. "I have *literal* firepower, and I can read her mind before she even *thinks* of doing anything. Now stop faffing about and get that thing on the lift."

We wrestled the thing in. The doors slid closed on Poppy and Jessica standing in the hallway. The machinery clanked, and the elevator lurched into motion. Down, down, down we went.

"So," Berron said. His voice was muffled, half-blocked by the Mirror, but still cheerful in a gallows humor kind of way. "What are the odds Daniel betrayed us?"

I closed my eyes, inhaled. Opened them. Exhaled. "He didn't," I said firmly.

I could have sworn there was no oxygen left by the time we got to the ground floor.

17

If I thought it was forever to get the Mirror down and out, it was two forevers waiting for Poppy to ride down with Jessica.

At last, the elevator dinged. The doors slid open. Poppy and Jessica stood next to each other. Jessica's all-black outfit looked stark next to Poppy's bright green and yellow.

I'd forgotten we were all still wearing our costumes. Berron, in that dramatic greatcoat with capes, all white, edged with black. Me in my purple thief getup. Come to think of it, I was actually stealing something. Well, stealing it *back*, really.

"After you," Poppy said to Jessica, politely, but with an I'll-flame-you-if-I-must edge.

Berron and I lifted the Mirror and headed outside. The dark lobby gave way to the weather we'd left behind, hot and humid, but with the sunlight draining from the streets like the tide going out.

"Now what?" Berron said.

I hadn't thought that far. But this was New York City, after all, and anything was possible.

Poppy was already on it, dragging Jessica along as she called to some workmen next to a nearby truck. "Pardon me—yes, *you* sir—may I hire your vehicle to transport this antique?"

The workman nudged his companion, not even needing to say, *Get a load of this tall broad with the funny accent.* He smiled. "*Hire* it? I ain't never heard of no 'hiring' a vehicle."

Poppy reached into a pocket, pulled out several hundreds, and waved them around. "Have you ever heard of dollars? Bucks? Greenbacks? How about dead presidents?"

He touched his cap. "Come to think of it, I may have heard of that, after all." He hooked his thumbs into his overall straps. "Where you want that thing to go, miss?"

Poppy turned back to me. "Where do we want it to go?"

"Your place." It was that or Victorine's, and as much as I trusted her, I was done outsourcing the Mirror to anyone else. Poppy had told me she had some magical security in place, too. If it was anything like the spell on the dancing statue at the LWW, I'd sleep better with the Mirror under our roof.

"I can only take one of youse up front," the workman added.

"I'll go," Jessica said.

Poppy elbowed her sharply. "Ha ha, what a card my dear friend is! Zelda, do you want to—"

"You go," I said. "The three of us will ride in the back." I didn't like having to keep an eye on the Mirror *and* Jessica, but between Berron and I, we should be able to handle it. We carefully loaded the Mirror into the cargo area, padding it as best we could with the stolen tablecloth.

"One sec," Berron said. He darted to a nearby planter, plunged his hand into the dirt, and came up holding an entire bush, roots and dirt and all.

"What the hell are you doing?" I said. "Daniel's lost who knows where, we're hauling a hot mirror, and you're *gardening*?"

"Trust me," he said. Then he turned to Jessica, gesturing gallantly with one arm while holding the plant in the other. "Ladies first."

Jessica climbed into the back of the truck. I followed. Berron came up last, and the truck driver closed the door. I instantly ignited a flame in both hands, both to see by and to keep Jessica in line. Berron put the plant at Jessica's feet.

She sneered at the scraggly bush. "What is that—"

Tendrils exploded outward.

The plant grew in a shimmering burst of green and gold magic, faster than possible, like a time-lapse video on maximum speed. Hundreds of tiny branches enclosed Jessica from the neck down, before she could even manage to squeak a protest.

It didn't stop her from protesting after the fact. You could tell how thrilled she was by the number of bad words she was using and the volume at which they came out. Good thing we were already moving and the sound of the truck rattling down the street covered all of it.

"Nice," I said to Berron.

He made a seated bow from the other side of the Mirror.

"You could have covered her mouth, though."

"Where's the fun in that?"

"Good point."

We were both silent as the truck rumbled on. What could be said in front of Jessica? Nothing we didn't want eventually making its way back to Prospero, when we let her go. I mean, it wasn't like we could keep her. It wasn't like with James, who had already been looking for a way out that night at the Vespers Club. But I had some ideas of what to do while we *could* keep her. Ideas for getting Prospero to spill what was going on with the Mirror. With the Forest of Emeralds.

We couldn't keep her for that long, though. She'd be missed. And it wasn't like we had a lot of extra space to keep her, not with Aunt Belinda visiting.

I groaned, rested my head on my arms. Aunt Belinda. I'd forgotten about my visitor. We were bringing a hostile vampire home to *Aunt Belinda*.

"What?" Berron said.

"Nothing."

"Liar."

Jessica had gone quiet, apparently having run out of her very large store of curse words, and was watching us as if she were a feral cat in a trap.

"Remember my aunt? The one who's helping with the restaurant? She's at home."

Berron smiled. "Is that all? Why worry? Old ladies love me."

I guffawed.

"What?" He looked slightly hurt.

I wiped a tear from my eyes. "I wasn't worried about you, you idiot. I was worried about introducing our new friend." I nodded toward Jessica.

She turned her head away with a disdainful sniff.

The truck rolled on, and Berron patted the Mirror like it was a nervous dog on the way to the vet.

Finally, we stopped. Berron gestured at the plant, which shrank to its original size in another burst of magic. Doors opened and slammed. The cargo lock tumbled and clanked, then the door rolled upward with a loud racket.

Our driver stood outside, smiling and holding out a business card. "Pleasure to do business with youse guys. You ever need anything special moved"—here he paused, meaningfully—"youse just give me a call."

"Thank you, kind sir," Poppy said, relieving him of the card and dropping a small curtsy. "Now, if we could?" She gestured to the Mirror.

"Of course," the driver said, backing away. "I'll leave youse to it."

Berron and I got the Mirror out while Poppy kept an eye on Jessica. This was the trickiest part, out in the street where visible magic couldn't be performed without exposing ourselves. The world of magic was still secret, after all—even if sometimes it seemed like a boiling pot under a bubbling lid.

Even carrying the Mirror and watching Jessica out of the corner of my eye, my list of worries whirled in my head. *Daniel. The Forest of Emeralds. The Arcade. Prospero. The Mirror.* Round and round it went, an endless series of tickets on the pass-through.

Sometimes you have to shut it all out and concentrate on what's in the pan *right now*.

We got up the front steps and I shifted the weight to Berron so I could fumble for my keys. Better me than Poppy, who couldn't take her eyes off Jessica, not here, not where it would be so easy to bolt. I almost had the key in the lock when Jester bounced into view in the front window, barking enthusiastically.

Then the lock turned and the door was flung open to reveal Aunt Belinda holding a leaping Jester on leash. Georgiana, the more relaxed of the two dogs, simply lifted her head from her usual position on the couch, her large dark eyes opening with mild interest.

Home smelled good: dogs, lemon polish, lingering bacon I'd cooked that morning.

"Shoot, girl, what you got there? You doing some redecorating?" It didn't take more than a second for the other shoe to drop, as she realized what we were carrying. "Oh, lordy. You all best get inside *quick*." She stepped back and Berron and I moved the Mirror through the doorway into the living room. "Hey, there, Poppy!" she added. "Who's this? She in that play y'all dressed up for?"

Jessica made an exasperated noise as Poppy prodded her inside.

"Um, not exactly—" Poppy began.

Aunt Belinda wasn't really listening. She addressed Jessica. "I'm Belinda. Belinda Campbell. But everybody just calls me 'Mama.'" She held her hand out.

Jessica eyed it like it was a snake.

"What's wrong with her? She don't talk or shake hands?"

Poppy opened her mouth to speak, but Berron interrupted. "Ma'am? I thought you were 'Aunt' Belinda?"

"Well, to my niece Zelda I am, 'cause it would get confusing otherwise."

"I would have thought you were sisters." He smiled.

She gave him a once-over. "You're a good-looking boy, but you ain't half as charming as you think you are."

Berron looked like he'd been shot.

I covered a snort of laughter with my hand. "Aunt Belinda, this is Jessica. She's one of the Blessed. From the crew that caused all that damage to the shop."

Aunt Belinda's face darkened like a wrinkly thundercloud. "Is that right? I'm glad I didn't shake your hand," she said to Jessica.

"Who cares?" Jessica muttered.

"*Pardon me?*" my aunt said, enunciating each word like a whip crack.

"Whatever," said the heedless Jessica.

"Right," Aunt Belinda said, firmly. She handed Jester's leash to Poppy.

Jester dashed back and forth, wild with excitement for visitors but too confused to choose between his beloved Berron and the fun new lady who smelled like steak.

Aunt Belinda cracked her knuckles. Cold air smashed through the room and picked Jessica right off her feet.

"Hey!" Jessica cried out. "Put me down."

"Apologize for that sass mouth of yours and I'll think about it," Aunt Belinda said. She moved her hands upward and thumped Jessica's head on the ceiling.

"Ow!" Jessica threw her hands up like an upside-down handstand.

"Ain't nobody mess with my family," Aunt Belinda continued. "Not 'less they want to get their hinders kicked, if you know what I mean."

"All right. All right! Let me down."

"What's that magic word, missy?" Another hand motion made Jessica spin in slow circles like a helium balloon caught in a draft.

"Please? I'm sorry?"

Aunt Belinda stopped the motion and looked Jessica square in the eye. "Don't try me, you hear?"

Jessica nodded rapidly.

Slowly, slowly, Aunt Belinda lowered Jessica over the couch, where she landed in the space not occupied by Georgiana.

This was all too much for Jester. He surged forward and popped the leash right out of Poppy's grip. He dashed across the room, ears flying, toenails skittering on the floor, and leaped onto the couch.

Or, more accurately, onto Jessica, who shrieked. Probably thinking she was being attacked by a furry demon.

I rushed forward, in case she tried to hurt him—but when the tornado of black fur revealed himself to be only a silly miniature poodle trying to kiss her face, she dropped her head into her hands.

And cried.

Jester, ever helpful, licked her tears as fast as they fell.

18

Jessica, vicious vampire, near-murderer, soaking my poodle with saltwater. She paused to tip her head back, blot around her eyes with the backs of her hands in an attempt to stop the impressively thick layer of liner and mascara from running down her cheeks. It kind of worked—instead of running down in streams, it blotched across her cheeks like soot on a chimney sweep.

Even Berron, ever-ready to kick the Blessed when they were down, didn't crack wise.

Georgiana heaved a great, doggy sigh, as if she'd had enough excitement for one day. Then she got up and resettled in the armchair, where she didn't fit and her front legs hung over the arm.

"Poppy," I said.

Poppy, who had been staring with her mouth slightly open at the scene on the couch, came back to herself. "Hm?"

"Can you and Berron go look for Daniel, please? You know where he would have come through." I wasn't going to say it, in front of Jessica, just in case. "Aunt Belinda and I will handle"—I paused, gestured at the Blessed and the poodle—"this. And Berron," I added. "If you try to say you need to stay here and protect me, *you* will be the one who needs protection. From me."

He ran his hand through his hair. "I didn't even say anything—"

"Out."

He slid past me, but in doing so, his hand brushed my shoulder. "Be careful," he murmured.

Berron and Poppy exited, leaving Aunt Belinda and I with the dogs and Jessica.

"Well, your life is just plum interesting, ain't it?" Aunt Belinda said.

"Tell me about it."

Though we hadn't seen each other in ages, the moment we were left alone with Jessica, the unspoken communication between us shifted. It became a family wavelength, the way all the holidays and family gatherings take on the same rhythm after years of repetition. Like a dish you can make without looking at the recipe. You know what to do without thinking about it.

I knew to step back and let Aunt Belinda make the first move.

Aunt Belinda leaned slightly forward and put her hands on her thighs, like a grown-up making themselves smaller to talk to a child. "Jessica? That your name?"

Jessica nodded, still not making eye contact.

"Now, you gotta stop all that crying, girl. How're we supposed to understand what's going on when you're making all them waterworks? Zelda, get her a Kleenex."

"I can't—the dog'll eat them."

"Is there anything that dog *won't* eat?"

"No."

Aunt Belinda hung her head and sighed.

"It's okay," Jessica piped up unexpectedly, collecting herself. "I can use my shirt." Possibly the first words she'd ever used with me that weren't rude, threatening, or theatrical.

Aunt Belinda straightened up and caught my eye, seeming to communicate that I should jump in.

So I did. I grabbed a chair and pulled it closer to the couch. Then I sat, my knees almost close enough to bump into Jessica's. Close to grab Jester if he took it into his empty head to try to chew on the decorative steel chain hanging from her waistband.

"You don't have to pretend you care," she said.

I reeled back. "Are you *serious*? If I showed up at your boss's place in tears, how long would I last?"

She looked away.

"Damn right." I let that hang in the air.

Jester, who had apparently reached his limit on salt licking, flopped across Jessica's lap and looked up at her expectantly.

"He wants you to pet him," I said. Unnecessarily, to my mind, because anyone looking at his large brown puppy eyes could tell that.

She still hadn't looked at me directly. She lifted her hand slowly, brought it down on Jester's velvety fur with a surprisingly soft touch.

Jester blinked contentedly and rolled half on his side.

"He wants a tummy rub," Aunt Belinda said helpfully.

"I'm not stupid," muttered Jessica, but it was so quietly delivered that even Aunt Belinda didn't take offense.

This close to her, I got a better look at her makeup-smudged face. Closer than I'd ever been before, really. And there was something I hadn't expected—

The melted mascara and eyeliner settled into fine lines around the corners of her eyes.

Crow's feet?

That was impossible. She'd been converted barely on the far side of eighteen.

Her head flew up like she'd felt my gaze. "What are you looking at?"

"Nothing—"

"You were staring." Her eyes challenged me, but her fingers continued to give Jester the light scritchy-scratchies he loved.

And that was the second thing: her hands.

I hadn't had what anyone would call beautiful hands in many, many years. Whatever soft skin I'd started with had gone rough early, what with working in kitchens from a young age, accumulating bumps and scrapes and burns and nicks. Tiny scars, a roadmap from kitchen recruit to seasoned officer. I didn't mind it. These were hands that did things.

But if Jessica's hands had retained her teenage youth, they wouldn't have had those telltale lines around the knuckles. The papery look rather than smooth satin.

Jessica was *aging*.

Which was impossible for a vampire. They turned age-*less*, not ag-*ed*. Victorine was at least a hundred years older than Jessica, and her hands were soft as rising bread dough.

Jessica lifted her hands from Jester, who looked betrayed, and held them out. "I see you noticed."

Aunt Belinda had been watching all this silently, her keen, ice blue eyes on the two of us. "Noticed what?"

"She's aging," I said.

Aunt Belinda let out a slow whistle. "I thought you all weren't supposed to do that. I mean, I ain't got none of you as friends, but that's what I heard."

Jessica eyed her, reassessing in the light of being smacked against the ceiling. "'Mama,' is it?"

Aunt Belinda smiled like the Florida sun. "That's me."

"Well, Mama," Jessica continued, returning to patting Jester with slow strokes down his back. "I was eighteen forever. At the price of"—she shrugged—"everything. And now it's gone."

"It's not *gone*. Is it?" I looked her over again. "You're still youthful."

"Not for long."

I remembered what Poppy had said, that Jessica was afraid of wrinkles. Sure, wrinkles weren't fun. Jessica valued her looks. But so did I, and wrinkles didn't make me cry. This was something else. Something more. A greater kind of grief.

I gasped. "You didn't—you haven't—"

Her plucked eyebrows rose as she waited for me to finish.

"You're losing your *power*?"

Her silence was confirmation.

"But *how*?"

Jessica made a dark sound of amusement, found an itchy spot behind Jester's ear, and scratched lightly while Jester's tongue lolled with happiness. "How do you think? Your boyfriend."

I was too shocked to correct her. "*Daniel*?"

"I don't know what he did to me. But after that day, nothing has ever been the same. I wake up more tired every day."

I sat back in my chair. *Daniel*. What did any of this mean? "Did you tell Prospero?" I asked.

"Why would I? So he could get rid of me that much sooner?"

"He would kill you for losing your power?"

She shot me an are-you-stupid look. "I mean *dismiss* me. How do you think we get by—the Blessed who aren't fabulously wealthy? We live on the patronage of Lord Prospero. Or Lady Victorine. Or those like them. You don't have any career prospects when you don't age. You can't stay in one place long enough. Inherited wealth is where it's at."

I thought of Berron. He got by on odd woodworking jobs—but probably only because he had a secret castle to retreat to. Real estate, man. It all came down to real estate.

"Although he might kill me," she mused, "if he thought I came with you voluntarily." She kissed Jester's head. Then she looked at me with a slightly unbalanced smile. "But you're the 'good' guys. Aren't you supposed to help people? You can help *me*."

My jaw dropped. "Help you? What do you want help with? Job placement? Or getting your powers back so you can return to doing what you do best? You know—sucking the life out of people?"

"Unfair," she purred.

"*Very* fair. You nearly killed Daniel! If I hadn't done some fancy footwork, he'd be in a box right now." Not, I thought, in whatever dimension he had currently disappeared to. I had to hope Poppy and Berron had a handle on that.

Aunt Belinda was right. My life was interesting. *Too* interesting. I couldn't trust Jessica not to stab us all in the back at the first sign of fortune reversing. But if the magic of the Blessed was implicated in what was happening in the Forest of Emeralds—

Jessica could be useful.

"How long can you be away before Prospero starts to suspect something?" She opened her mouth to answer, but I interrupted. "Before you answer, remember I can get Poppy back here to make sure you're not lying."

"I have left for several days at a time without telling him where I was going."

I looked at her, trying to read the truth in her eyes. Jester looked at her, too, but only because she had briefly stopped petting him.

"You know," Aunt Belinda said, addressing Jessica out of nowhere. "Zelda started over at your age. Picked up and moved with nothing but her old car and her dog."

"Sold that car on the way into town," I added.

Aunt Belinda nodded. "Worked hard, didn't you, Zel? Renovating that old restaurant. Putting in the hours. Putting in the sweat."

"I had help." I smiled a little, thinking of the early days with Berron and Daniel. Lily giving Jester the spa treatment. Moving in with Poppy and Georgiana. Even sparring with Victorine.

"You may think you're old," Aunt Belinda continued, to Jessica, "but you ain't halfway there. You got time for dreams, yet." She patted Jessica's knee. "Only you know what those dreams will be."

"My dreams are blood."

"Bull," Aunt Belinda shot back. "Acting spooky don't fool me. Your dreams are being in control of things. Zelda here knows a thing or two about that." Jessica and I shared an uncomfortable look, and Aunt Belinda cackled. "Everybody thinks I'm some old lady with a funny accent who don't know her butt from a hole in the ground. I know what's up. I been doing magic since before the two of you were *born*." She held out her hand. Out of nowhere, a black crow landed on her outstretched hand. Its flapping wings, as it steadied itself, trailed silver magic.

"Is that your familiar?" I said. "What's its name again?"

"Crow," she said, with a fond smile. "Just 'Crow.' I ain't bothering with no fancy names."

Jessica looked between us like we'd lost our minds. "What crow? What are you talking about?"

"Crow, here," Aunt Belinda said, ignoring the interruption, "is going to help you."

"There's nothing there—"

"Au contraire." Aunt Belinda's Southern accent mangled the French into something else entirely. "This here's my loyal familiar. He's special, this one. He can go far away from me. And I can see anything he sees."

Apprehension wrinkled up Jessica's crow's feet. "So?"

"So he's going to keep an eye on you for a while. Till you decide what your dreams are gonna be." Aunt Belinda nodded to me. "My niece here'll get regular reports."

"You're going to *watch* me?"

"We may be 'good,'" Aunt Belinda said. "But we ain't *stupid*."

Crow cocked his head and fixed Jessica with a beady-eyed stare.

"I'll call Victorine," I said. "See if she can put Jessica up, since we're out of beds."

"Maybe you should think about changing that weird outfit you got on before you go running through the streets," Aunt Belinda said.

I waved the suggestion away. I needed to find Daniel, outfit be damned.

I had even more questions now.

19

Victorine seemed amused that I'd ended up stealing a second member of Prospero's gang.

"I didn't steal James," I said, speed-walking through the Upper West Side on my way to Central Park. "He walked of his own free will."

"'Walked?' As I recall, it was more like 'running' and 'trying not to get killed.'"

"Hilarious," I said. Night was falling. The temperature was dropping. I didn't want to stumble through the North Woods in the dark, not because of crime—New York was safer than it had ever been, and my magic could blast any mortal threat to shreds—but because I didn't need to twist a knee or ankle on a tree root in the dark.

"Who will she swear allegiance to?"

"You, I assumed."

"James would have a fit," she said, with the perfect calm of someone who didn't care whether someone had a fit or not, because he would do as he was told.

"It's not like she's going to swear allegiance to *me*."

"You don't want to add to your collection?"

I scoffed. "My collection?"

"Daniel is an excellent start—but you could use someone truly ruthless in your organization."

"I don't *have* an organization. I have a sandwich shop. And I prefer 'can keep their station clean' to 'ruthless,' thanks very much."

"Jessica would make an excellent asset. Put to the right use."

"You take her then. She can be your brand-new, murder-y pal. You can practice your killing techniques in that underground bunker of yours." I paused. "Although she didn't actually *say* she was changing sides. Just that she wanted help."

"So she's still Prospero's."

"For now. I have to return her in a few days, before she's missed."

In the silence, I could almost see her taking a blithe sip of her signature green tea, the one that smelled of apples. "If Prospero finds out," she said, "he won't take this well."

"No kidding." I jaywalked Central Park West when the traffic cleared. "That's why he can't find out."

"You're a business owner. You should know all bills come due, eventually."

Boy, did I know it. Secrets, lies, promises, curses: they all fluttered like tickets in the pass, vicious little orders waiting to be dealt with.

In the distance, coming down the sidewalk from the opposite direction, a flash of bright yellow and green. The crowd eased apart and revealed an Othello cookie of clothing: black on one side, white on the other.

Yellow and green—Poppy.

White jacket with black piping—Berron.

And a black jacket with a red lining. *Daniel*.

I came to a full stop in the middle of the sidewalk, causing annoyed New Yorkers to swerve around me.

"Zelda?" said Victorine.

"I'll talk to you later." I hung up.

Daniel. I should have run to him. Run *at* him. Shaken him. Yelled at him. But I couldn't move, because I had double vision. I saw someone I trusted. Someone I didn't trust.

Someone I knew. Someone I didn't.

Secrets. Lies. Promises. Curses.

This had to end.

I'd tell him we had Jessica. He'd admit to everything, tell me what he had been doing that day, meeting her in the Puerto Rican restaurant. I'd cop to the fact that I'd followed him there. Everything would be out in the open again, sunlight instead of shadows. No more games.

I straightened up. Stuffed my phone in my back pocket.

Then I strode to meet them.

"Daniel Palmer, where have you been?" I punched his bicep, not gently. "And what the hell were you thinking?"

"First of all, *ow*." He rubbed his arm. "Second of all—nice to see you, too."

"It's all right," Berron said to Daniel. "She hits me too."

"Both of you hush," Poppy said. "Zelda, he says he fell *all the way through*."

"All the way where?"

"From one flower field to the other. Nothing in between." Her words were precise, neutral. That didn't fit. Poppy was one to get excited. If her voice was neutral, it meant she didn't believe him.

I looked at Daniel. "You've been lying in the North Woods this whole time?" I cringed inside as soon as the words left my mouth. *Lying*. Why did I pick that word?

"Yeah," he said, slowly. "It did something to me, going through. I got really dizzy, had to lie down in the grass until it passed." He rubbed a hand over his head. "I'm still unsteady, to be honest."

Berron observed all this with almost unholy-looking amusement. Figured. He was just the type of weirdo to enjoy watching someone lie.

Then again, so was I. I couldn't judge.

Where *had* Daniel been? Had he actually visited the Arcade? Would he tell me if he had?

Of course he would.

Right?

He had fallen straight through. No stops. Gotten dizzy. Laid down until Poppy and Berron picked him up. I could believe that. We were about to be all in the open again, weren't we?

Here goes nothing. "We have Jessica," I said, watching him very closely.

His eyebrows rose. "Jessica? Why?"

This was where he was supposed to tell *me* what was going on.

Instead, he waited politely for me to keep talking.

I looked at Poppy, who didn't need to read my mind to know what I was thinking. "Because..." My brain froze over like the Mirror. Why wasn't he confessing? "Because she was there when we got out of the Mirror." I didn't explain about Prospero's, not yet, not until I heard whatever information Daniel gave away freely.

Daniel frowned. "She tried to kill me, Zelda. And now you want to—what? Adopt her like a stray cat? Isn't that dangerous?"

I wanted to shout: *If she's so dangerous, why were you getting mofongo with her?* Instead, I said: "I'm not adopting her. I'm borrowing her. We have to get her back before her boss notices she's gone."

"And she's going to go along with this? Why?" Poppy had been out of range of Daniel, out of politeness, but now she was shuffling closer. Daniel turned and gave her a look. "Poppy, I like you, but back off."

Poppy reddened and retreated.

"What's the matter?" Berron said to Daniel. "Got something to hide?"

"If you weren't immune you'd be skipping away like a schoolgirl," Daniel shot back.

Berron shrugged without an ounce of shame.

Wind kicked up, coming in off the river, cooling the sweat that threatened to drip down my spine. There were a lot of factors here, but it couldn't be any worse than coordinating Sunday brunch for a table of ten. Daniel might be a master of the universe, but I was still in charge. Still on top.

It would take more than a rich, lying, red-eyed, hot-looking vampire to throw off my game.

"I'll explain everything," I said. "Back at the restaurant."

Daniel exhaled, ran his hands over his head again, causing his long jacket to flare as he raised his arms, revealing the red lining. "Okay."

"Come on," I said, to everyone. "Dinnertime."

We were a strange parade, still in our costumes on the walk back to West Side Sandwiches. No one blinked an eye. This was New York. It would take more than funny outfits to turn heads.

Yellow streetlights glowed above us and headlights whipped past us. When you lost the daytime details, sounds became that much louder: horns honking, buses hissing, people shouting directions and greetings and orders.

The restaurant shone in the darkness like home. James had the closing shift, of course. Leave it to the Blessed to stay up late. I opened the door and the smell of bread and meat and cheese swept into the street. My mouth watered; it had been a long time since I ate. I could only imagine that Poppy felt the same.

And Daniel, in a different way.

Berron, on the other hand, seemed to exist on hot beverages and stolen apples.

There was a brief hang-up as both Berron and Daniel attempted to hold the door.

"It's all right, boys," I said. "I'll hold the door. It's my restaurant."

Poppy breezed in. "Thank you, madam!"

"Strong *and* charming," Berron said, lightly brushing my cheek with a long finger as he crossed the threshold.

Daniel rolled his eyes, and I did the same.

We both chuckled.

Peace, for a moment. I let the door close behind me with a jangle of bells. The restaurant had emptied out, as it usually did at this time of night.

James had cranked up the radio while going through closing procedures. Sounded like the Stone Temple Pilots. "What's shaking?" he called.

"Party of four, James. Join us when you can. I'm gonna set everyone up." Nothing says normal like putting on an apron and wielding a knife, even if that knife had wielded more power in one afternoon than most of us see in a lifetime. I stored it in its special sheath and locked it away when I wasn't wearing it, so it took unlocking the box and unbuttoning the sheath to get at it.

I tried to keep it businesslike, not stop and stare at the beautiful blade and handle, but I failed every time. The sharp steel flashed like the lightning over the Forest of Emeralds. How could I not stare? My thumb rubbed the handle one more time, with appreciation, before I turned to the task at hand.

What would everyone want?

I could ask, but where was the challenge in that?

First Poppy. Didn't matter if it was technically dinnertime—Poppy liked sweet stuff. The sign in her kitchen said *Eat Dessert First*, after all. I had some leftover gluten-free apple tart and some vanilla ice cream hanging around. I cut a slice of the tart and threw it in the oven to warm.

Next, Berron. I turned on my little espresso machine, then set up the portafilter, tamper, and a demitasse cup and saucer. Caffeine seemed to have absolutely no effect on him, no matter what time of day he consumed it. I envied that.

And finally Daniel. There was a discreet lunchbox stored here, too, but it felt wrong to offer only something that set him apart from the rest of us. So I laid out a thick slice of bread and topped it with some warmed-up mashed potatoes, shredded pot roast, and a healthy—or, not-so-healthy—scoop of gravy. Gravy probably had no effect on a vampire's cholesterol.

James maneuvered past me as he continued to clean up. "Making anything for yourself?"

"Not hungry yet." In a night full of falsehoods, that was another one. But it was more like a way of not having to explain: I didn't want to eat until I could relax. And I definitely wasn't relaxed yet.

I plated everything and loaded it onto a tray: Poppy's tart, with ice cream and some whipped cream; Berron's espresso, topped with whipped cream, making it an espresso con panna; and Daniel's sandwich with a side of his... preferred beverage.

"Ooh," said Poppy, delightedly, as I placed the tart in front of her.

Berron licked a bit of whipped cream from his cup, a dark-eyed prince turned small child when confronted with fluffy dairy products.

Daniel regarded the open-faced sandwich with something like surprise.

"What?" I said. "You don't like it?" I picked up the plate again. "I can make something else."

"No!" he said, placing his hand on my wrist. "No, it's perfect. Thank you. I just wasn't expecting—food."

I lowered the plate with care and set the sandwich in front of him, next to the diner coffee cup filled with something we wouldn't talk about if we could avoid it. "You always told me pot roast was your comfort food."

He fumbled with the fork and knife, more human now than I'd seen him in ages. When he looked down at his plate, you couldn't see the red in his eyes.

James locked the door and joined us, flipping a chair around to sit backwards, using the back of the chair as an armrest.

I set the tray aside and took the empty seat at the head of the table.

Time to figure out what the hell was going on.

20

The four of them looked at me like I had a plan. I wished I had a plan. Instead, I looked toward the window, with the name "West Side Sandwiches" backwards and silhouetted across the glass, and for a moment, I saw my grandmother standing there.

Not literally—the only ghost was the ghost in my own mind—but real, the way that some memories are so strong they feel like a presence.

She had just closed up shop for the night, and she took a last look out the window, a survey of the sidewalk and the street and the buildings that stretched the length of them. A queen looking out from the ramparts of her castle. How funny that she reigned over this normal, real-world place, while living a secret life. Balancing ordinary and the fantastic. Magic and the mundane.

Spells and sandwiches.

Ah, Grandma. How did you do it?

I dragged my gaze from the window, folded my hands on the table, and leaned in. "All right. Everything we know." I recounted the red magic I'd found in the Forest of Emeralds.

"Prospero, obviously," James said.

"Thank you for your input, James. I wasn't finished." I described where the Mirror had sent us the second time through, for the benefit of James and Daniel, who hadn't been there.

James smirked. "Prospero."

"What we don't know," I went on, "is why."

"Given enough time, you tick everyone off, don't you?" James said.

"Do you *want* to keep your job?"

He raised his hands.

I gave him a long stare before I continued. "While we were inside, the Mirror ended up at Prospero's."

James, unable to stop himself, crowed with triumph. "I told you!"

"Prospero *stole* the Mirror while we were inside," Poppy added.

That only made James look more smug. "He was trying to get rid of you."

It had been easy to avoid thinking about it, in the heat of the moment. Easy to concentrate on the problem at hand—getting out—and not the cold truth. If we hadn't escaped, if we'd been stuck in that silent, black-and-white world...

Nope.

Wasn't going to think about it.

I shook it off. "Why would Prospero want rid of us? I mean, I know he hates me, personally. I know he wanted to seal the Gentry inside the Mirror. But let's pretend we're him. Why are we so important? What is he trying to do that he thinks we would stop?"

Poppy sat up taller. Her eyes lit, and her face, always so bright to begin with, nearly glowed from the sharp joy of solving a puzzle. She began ticking her fingers one by one. "First and foremost, he wants the Gentry out of the way, and you showed him that you weren't going to be on his side. If you're not with him, you're against him. Right?" She waited for my nod before she continued. "Right. Secondly, he stole the Mirror. Thirdly, there are traces of red magic in the Gentry's field of flowers. Correct?"

"Correct," Berron said. He tipped his cup upside down in search of one more drop of cream-swirled espresso.

"But you're missing something," Poppy continued. "You're not putting all of those things together. I mean, not *you*, personally, but all of us. So far."

Daniel leaned back and crossed his arms.

Poppy picked up her fork, gestured with it. "Think about it. If he really wanted to trap the Gentry, why didn't he just *smash the Mirror*?"

The rest of us looked at each other. I hoped they felt as stupid as I did for missing the obvious.

"What's the point of trying to get you to lock it? Why *steal* it? One blow"—she swung the fork through the air—"and *smash*! Problem solved. But it isn't," she said, with obvious satisfaction. "Because, yes, he wants the Gentry out of the way. But he still needs the Mirror."

"For what?" Daniel said.

Poppy raised the fork. "Aha! Now we're getting somewhere." She leaned in. "It's *traveling*. All of it. Through the Mirror. Through the flowers. He wants out. He wants to *escape*."

"Escape," James breathed.

"Precisely," Poppy said, with a final fork flourish. "Prospero thinks the Mirror is how the Blessed will finally escape from the island of Manhattan." Speech finished, she dug into the apple tart with its rapidly melting pool of ice cream.

"Um, *where* did you say the Mirror was now?" James said, looking at me.

"Poppy's. We stole it back."

"I hope you have good security."

Poppy swallowed her bite. "The best. The League of Women's Welfare—the Ladies Who Witch—installed it. It's never been activated, of course. But I'm told it would create quite an impressive display."

"You think the Mirror could actually be used to leave Manhattan?" Daniel asked.

"I don't know," Poppy said. "But it's a theory."

Daniel had always been good at looking calm when he wasn't—but I had the feeling that if he thought he could get away with it, he would have bolted for the door and run all the way to Poppy's townhouse.

As always, Berron took all of it in, a great prince who collected other people's weaknesses like a squirrel collected nuts.

"And there's the other thing," I said, not looking at James. "Well, not thing. Person." I cleared my throat. "We took Jessica."

"You *what*?" James said.

"She was at Prospero's. With the Mirror. So we made her come with us."

James—instead of shouting at me—sat there with his mouth open.

I would have preferred the shouting.

"You—"

I still didn't look at him.

"You took. Jessica. From Prospero's." He paused. "Are you *insane*?"

"It was for the best," I said. I wasn't ready to share about Jessica's power fading. Not yet.

"'For the best,' she says!" James stood up, spun the chair away, began pacing. "I wasn't *important* to him. I didn't *want* to be there. He'd still end me if he had the chance! And you took *Jessica*." He threw his hands up.

"She say she needs our help—"

James laughed. "You're more of a simpleton than I thought."

I pushed back from the table and stood up, feeling the low tide of the magic in my veins suddenly rise as if pulled by a full moon. "Maybe I am a simpleton, James. But maybe you weren't there, today, when I saw a child asleep under the roots of a dying apple tree. A child who will never wake up if we don't figure out what's going on and how to stop it. That's all I want. I don't care who I have to pull in—the Naked Cowboy, or Yoko Ono, or the Blessed who used Daniel as an afternoon snack. I will fix this if it kills me. I will go through whoever I have to." I met Daniel's gaze then.

He was unfazed. A slight nod, even, as if he understood.

What to make of that?

Poppy reached out, placed her hand over mine, where I had been gripping the table without realizing it, and gave it a gentle squeeze. She looked around the table, and then to James. "We all will," she said.

James stopped pacing. Looked sheepish, and retook his seat. "Well, yeah. I mean, I don't have it in for some poor kid under an apple tree."

Berron steepled his fingers on the table. Whatever amusement had been on his features before had disappeared. "What next?" he said, quietly.

I sat. "We need whatever we can get out of Jessica. James, you should be there."

He nodded.

"And then..." I paused, gathering my thoughts. "I'm going back to Prospero."

James and Daniel immediately protested.

Berron, for once, was silent. Watching.

"Listen to me," I said. "I *am* going back to Prospero. But not—" I stopped, considered who I trusted. Could I be sure not a single person at the table would betray me? It was a risk.

I decided to follow my instinct, the same instinct that told me when a roast beef was done. "But not as me," I finished. "As Jessica."

James looked impressed.

"Won't Prospero wonder why she disappeared?" Daniel asked.

"That's the only part of this that makes some sense," James said. "Jessica took off when she wanted. Within reason. She shouldn't be gone for too long, though."

Daniel looked me up and down. "You're going to need a new costume."

"I can handle that," I said, waving the worry away.

"No," Daniel said. "I mean, for the ball." Everyone looked at him. "The Royal Ball? The one Prospero's hosting at the next Vespers Club?"

"How did *you* hear about it?" I asked.

"Victorine. I'm—" He paused, cleared his throat. "I was going to tell you. I'm invited."

Poppy gasped.

Berron finally smiled. "And there it is."

"Quiet, you," I said to Berron, before returning to Daniel. "Why would you go to Prospero's party?"

"Why did *you* go to the Vespers Club?" he countered.

"For information..."

Daniel shrugged, like it had been obvious all along. "I thought I could help. So I got in touch with Jessica and got an invite so I could meet with Prospero."

"And neither of you thought this might be a good thing to mention to me? In case you—I don't know—got *killed* again?"

"I didn't know if it would work. I didn't want to get your hopes up." He took a long swig from his mug, started to wipe his reddened lips, then appeared to think better of it. Instead he cut a bite of bread from the open-faced pot roast sandwich and discreetly dabbed his lips before eating the bread.

He hadn't been about to betray me. He had been trying to help. And he didn't want to disappoint.

Furious love roared through me.

There are all kinds of love in the world, but the love that comes from trust restored is stronger than espresso, sweeter than ice cream, and more comforting than a boat of pot roast gravy.

21

As late as it was, even the borrowed magic flowing through me wasn't enough to stop the yawns. After we made our tentative plans, I locked up, and Poppy and I walked home to our dogs.

I owed Jester extra snuggles.

I was surprised to find Aunt Belinda still up. Not only up, but on her feet, arms crossed, staring out into the street. But there was no time to ask questions, at first—not with Jester bouncing up and down like a furry spring, trying to lick my face on the fly.

"Jester! Sit, boy. Sit!" Cue more jumping. "Want a treat? You gotta sit, boy." At last his butt hit the ground, although his tail was still wagging so hard his whole body vibrated, and I could tell that his willpower was already showing cracks. I grabbed a handful of freeze-dried liver treats from a nearby drawer. Doled them out one at a time, in exchange for *sit*, *shake*, and *down*, and my nutty poodle chilled out. A little.

Finally I was able to look up. Poppy and Georgiana had gone through to the kitchen.

Aunt Belinda was watching me. "You got him trained real good," she said.

I laughed. "Not really. But he tries." I looked around. "Where's Jessica?"

"I sent her to your room to lie down. Hitting your forties all at once is rough on a body. Don't worry, Crow's there, too. Jessica can't cause no trouble while Crow's got eyes on her." She looked at me speculatively. "You ain't got a familiar yet, have you?"

"It's complicated."

Aunt Belinda shook her head. "Ain't nothing that complicated." She gestured toward the window. "See that big ol' city out there? Lotta people are right scared of it. 'Too big,' they say. 'Too many people.' They don't realize it's just a bunch of little old small towns all smushed together, cozy-like. I ain't scared of it." She chuckled to herself. "But I do miss home. You know why?"

I picked up Jester and cradled him in my arms like a lamb. "The weather?"

"You ain't wrong, but no, girl. Not the weather. Sit down. I gotta talk to you."

When someone like Aunt Belinda says *sit*, you sit. I sat. Jester curled up on my lap.

"Back home I got friends and more friends. Witchy friends. Un-witchy friends. I got family, too. My daughter Luella. If I need help, all I gotta do is give the high sign and they all come running." She plopped in a chair and looked at me with her ice-blue eyes. "I see you got your friend Poppy." She nodded approvingly. "And that fellow who works for you. James. He seems all right. And those two gentleman callers—"

I accidentally inhaled my own spit and started coughing uncontrollably. Jester leaped up and barked at me, presumably because he thought I was barking too. "Daniel and Berron are not," I choked out, "gentleman callers."

"Whatever they are," Aunt Belinda said. "They seem pretty all right, too. But"—here she scooted forward on the seat of the chair, as if to emphasize the importance of what she was about to say—"when I was growing into my powers, I had my witch friends, Hilda and Queenie, to help me. Luella has her friends Rose and Pepper. We may use different elements, but we all have the same magic." She paused. "You're on your own up here. You ain't got nobody like you."

"Have you been talking to my mother?"

"That ain't neither here nor there."

I raised one eyebrow. "Uh-huh. Well, as much as I would like to learn from someone just like me, the last person with that quality was Grandma."

"Bless her soul," Aunt Belinda said.

"Yes. And I try to do what I think she might have done, under the circumstances. It isn't perfect, but it's what I've got. Here's the thing, though." I shifted. Jester had jumped to the top of the couch behind me and draped himself around my shoulders like an old-fashioned fur stole. "Everyone I'm friends with here has a different talent. Poppy's an elemental fire witch. My brother's got air magic, like you. Daniel, James, and Victorine are Blessed. Berron's one of the Gentry. All different. But they *all* teach me, in their own ways."

Aunt Belinda nodded slowly, seeming to consider what I said. "I suppose you just need a water witch and an earth witch to round out the set."

"Honestly, it would have been nice to have someone to show me how to use this mask." I tapped my face, to show where the mask sat.

"Artifacts are tricky. My friend Hilda gave one to her sister—the Key of Shadows—and the sister used it to cause all kinds of trouble." Aunt Belinda shook her head. "That woman popped in and out of reality like it was the 7-Eleven."

"In and out of reality?"

"From some other dimension."

My thoughts crashed like a line of taxis rear-ending each other at a sudden red light. "*What* other dimension?"

"Hilda said it was hush-hush. Not many people knew about it. Called it 'The Shadows.'"

"The Shadows," I repeated. Memories of the silent, black-and-white museum nearly blinded me to what was actually in front of me. I reached back to pat Jester's fuzzy fur, because it was the only thing soothing enough to pull me out of memories that sucked the air from my chest. "What did the Shadows look like? Did you ever see it?"

"My daughter's friend Pepper did. She talked all about it. Cold. No colors. No electricity. Real quiet, spooky even."

"Black and white?"

Aunt Belinda nodded.

"No lights?"

Aunt Belinda shook her head.

I cursed.

"New York ain't doing your vocabulary no good," she observed mildly.

"Who has the Key of Shadows now?"

"I didn't bring it with me, if that's what you're asking. It's back in Sparkle Beach, with Hilda. Or Miami, with her sister." Aunt Belinda tapped her chin thoughtfully, as if this would cause the Key to suddenly resolve itself in one location or another. "Why do you ask?"

"I think I may have been in the Shadows. Through there." I nodded toward the Mirror.

"Doesn't it go to fairy land?"

"It did—but there's something wrong with it. It's malfunctioning. Or booby-trapped. Or something. I don't know. It's complicated."

When Aunt Belinda smirked, her wrinkles went deep. "Ain't nothing that complicated."

I stopped myself from saying, *Wanna bet?* Instead I explained everything she hadn't heard, up to Jessica's arrival.

Aunt Belinda listened. When I finished, she said, "So you think someone sent you into the Shadows. On purpose."

I nodded.

"I'm right curious as to what Jessica would have to say about all this."

"I thought she was lying down."

Aunt Belinda stood. "She ain't gonna be. Y'all need answers."

Jester, always alert to something fun about to happen, jumped down to the floor and looked up at Aunt Belinda with shining brown eyes. When we headed for the stairs he streaked ahead, his tiny claws scrabbling on the wooden steps.

I knocked on the door as Aunt Belinda hovered behind me. "Jessica?" I said. "I'm coming in." The heavy wooden door opened on my own familiar bedroom—except instead of me, tucked in bed like I should have been, there was an unfamiliar lump buried under my covers, and a crow sitting on the headboard like a prop from a Vincent Price movie. "Hey. Jessica. Wake up."

A loud groan came from deep within the heap of pillow and blankets. *My* pillows and blankets. "Go away."

"Time to face the day. Well, the night," I amended.

Jessica buried herself deeper. "What are you, my mother?"

"If I were your mother I'd slap that sass right out o' your mouth," Aunt Belinda piped up.

"Aunt Belinda, you'd have died before you even *thought* of laying a hand on Luella. Don't be ridiculous."

Aunt Belinda landed a sharp elbow in my side. "Don't ruin the act," she muttered.

I rubbed my side and turned my attention back to the vampiress in my bed. "You can't stay here. There's no room."

"You can sleep on the couch, can't you?" Pouty *and* demanding. How charming.

"This is *my* room, princess. And it's where my aunt is sleeping. I'm already on the couch."

Another epic groan, as if she had been betrayed by the entire world.

"Dramatic, ain't she," said Aunt Belinda.

"Right." I dusted my hands, then strode forward. I seized the topmost edges of the blankets and hauled them downward in one big pull. "Up."

Exposed, Jessica curled tighter and kept her eyes squeezed shut, her straight black bob spread out like a mohawk on my pillow.

"Up!" I repeated, yanking my pillow out from under her head.

That got a growl instead of a groan. Progress. "Come on. You're getting out of my bed and going somewhere there's actually space for you. I'm taking you to Victorine's."

"She'll *murder* me," Jessica said, sounding more grumpy than afraid.

"Great. There'll be one less Blessed who tried to kill my ex-boyfriend."

That got her eyes open. She glared at me with something like... respect? Then it melted into a self-satisfied smile, the cat who not only ate the canary but tipped over the baby's milk bottle to wash it down. "Daniel and I were just playing."

I had to remind myself that we had taken her from Prospero's in order to have the advantage, and strangling her with my own two hands would remove that advantage. Instead, I seized her arm and pulled her upright.

"Hey, hey! Don't touch me, freak."

"Calm down. I don't steal powers, I just copy them. And why would I want *yours*, anyway?" It was an instinctive comeback, not even thought out, but it hit Jessica like a thrown stiletto. She stiffened, pulled away.

Don't feel sorry for her. Don't feel sorry for her.

Damn it, I felt sorry for her.

<h1 style="text-align:center">22</h1>

In case the townhouse was being watched, we took the secret back way out: onto the tiny second floor patio and down the fire escape into the alley connecting to the street behind us. Out on the sidewalk, Jessica's gaze skittered over every shift in the night-time illumination. Between passing cars, blinking signs, and the green-yellow-red stoplights, her eyes didn't stop moving from the moment we stepped outside Poppy's townhouse.

Neither of us spoke.

I didn't want to admit it, but I'd caught her mood. I spent the whole walk on high alert. Though I loved Central Park at night—especially since magic had taken over my life, giving me little to fear in the mortal realm—this midnight stroll was giving me a metallic taste for what it must have been like during the more lawless decades. Listening for footfalls behind you. Watching for shadows to step out of the woods.

The only comfort was Aunt Belinda's familiar. Crow followed us the entire way, flying from tree to tree, or gliding silently over open fields. What Crow saw, Aunt Belinda saw, and that reassured me.

We reached Victorine's street. With its pressure-washed sidewalks and facades, it was almost like a theme park version of New York in comparison to the more lived-in streets of the Upper West Side.

I took the steps to the front door only to realize that Jessica was still standing on the sidewalk, her arms crossed like she was cold. "You coming?"

"Yeah," she said, rubbing her arms one more time before joining me. Maybe not quite as brave as she put on.

I banged on the door.

Lights blazed behind the cut-glass windows.

The door opened, and a familiar face peeked out—Claudette, Victorine's housekeeper. "Miss Hawkins. Another late night visit, I see? And you've brought a visitor"—she yawned—"again. Miss Laguerre will be so pleased." She shuffled backward and opened the door wide enough for us to pass through.

"Thank you, Claudette. I hope you're doing well?" I said, feeling ridiculous trading pleasantries in the middle of the night, but figuring it was the least I could do after dragging the poor woman out of bed.

"Yes, opening the door at the witching hour is my hobby. Sometimes, I do it just for fun."

"Claudette, you're getting downright sassy. What would Miss Laguerre say?"

"Double my pay, probably." Claudette closed and locked the door.

"Who's that at this hour?" James said, his voice fading in as he came down the hall. "Middle of the freakin' night—" He froze as he saw Jessica standing in the foyer. "Oh." Then his expression went from vague annoyance to something like relish. "Well. Look who's here."

"I'll get Miss Laguerre," Claudette said, retreating upstairs.

"The prodigal Blessed," James said. "Zelda said you needed—what was it?" he asked, theatrically. "Ah, yes. Help. The great Jessica needs *help*."

Jessica had been hanging back, but she pushed past me to stalk further into the marble-floored foyer, where a mirror hung over a delicate side table. She touched her hair and straightened her clothes. "Go to hell, James."

James laughed. "I'm sorry, did someone say you were in *charge*, here? Because I don't recall getting that memo."

I clomped over to the two of them. My Doc Martens always seemed clunkier at Victorine's. "Lay off," I said. "She does need help. She's losing her powers."

James turned to me, thunderstruck. "What?" He looked at Jessica, who was still looking in the mirror. "For real?" He took her arm.

She shook him off. "Touch me again and I'll use whatever I have left to break every bone in your body."

"You have to tell me." He put his hands on his hips, shot me a look, then gestured toward Jessica. "Zelda, make her tell me."

"I don't know for sure. But she thinks it might have been Daniel."

"Daniel!" The look on his face veered between hope and disbelief before crash-landing on glee—at Jessica's obvious unhappiness. "So... your greedy bloodsucking got you in the end, did it?"

Jessica folded her arms and looked away.

"Was it worth it?" he said, hovering closer, clearly enjoying himself, not paying attention to the warning signs. "Did you enjoy your last 'meal'?"

Jessica unfolded with a raging shriek and launched herself at James. They landed on the marble floor so hard the chandelier rattled, and proceeded to roll through the foyer like a sideways tornado. Whatever Jessica lacked in raw power, she was making up for it with sheer anger—and a natural willingness to fight dirty.

I stumbled backward before I got knocked down. If I'd had a bucket of water, I would have thrown it on them. What *could* I use?

Poppy's fire magic? I didn't need to burn the two of them like toast.

Vampire strength? Wrestling James and Jessica—no thanks.

Aunt Belinda's air magic? Mine wasn't strong enough to hold the two of them.

Meanwhile they'd slammed into the side table and knocked a porcelain figure to the floor, where it instantly smashed into a zillion pieces.

At that moment, Victorine appeared above us on the final turn of the spiral staircase. She delicately cleared her throat.

James and Jessica rolled apart, huffing and puffing. James lay face-up, and he pointed at Jessica. "She started it."

Jessica scrambled to her feet and seized a nearby candlestick, raising it over James.

In a motion almost too fast to track, Victorine blurred down the stairs and had Jessica in a headlock, disarmed, before Jessica could even squeak. "Will you behave, Initiate?" she asked, mildly, loosening her grip just enough so Jessica could make a tiny nod. Victorine released her.

James got up, keeping his eyes on Jessica. The two of them stood uneasily, every weight shift crunching on the remains of the porcelain figure.

Victorine ignored them. "Zelda. How nice to see you again. I fear I meet you far too often in my bathrobe." She flicked at the plush collar, as if she'd just noticed she wasn't dressed to the nines. "Have you brought me another stray?"

"We don't have space at Poppy's right now—"

"Of course not." She glanced at James and Jessica, who were now both staring firmly at the floor. "And I already have the first toy in the set. Why not the second?" She descended, patted Jessica's cheek.

If that had been anyone else, Jessica would have bitten off a few fingers. Instead, she stood motionless, not daring to make eye contact.

"Zelda has had a long day," Victorine said. "I'm sure she needs her rest. Let us finish this and allow the night's peace to descend upon us all." She folded her hands, composed and formal. "Initiate, kneel."

There was a pause. No one moved, least of all Jessica, who kept her eyes downcast and remained absolutely still. It would have been very hard to kneel on those shards, but James would have done it, if told.

Then Jessica spoke so quietly I could barely hear her. "I cannot swear, Lady Victorine."

"Look at me, child."

Jessica lifted her gaze. Even now her eyes did not glow as red as they had before.

"You would abandon your Elder and choose no other? This is death. You know the Covenant."

Jessica's chin rose a fraction of an inch. "I abandon no one, Lady. I am"—her gaze dropped, and she swallowed—"I am in between. I belong to nothing. I am becoming human."

Hunger warmed James' face like a fire. Had Poppy been there, I had no doubt she would have seen his secret suburban dreams of picket fences and green lawns, adoring wife and growing family.

Victorine's elegant eyebrows rose. "This is not possible."

"I think this might take longer than a quick kneel-and-swear," I said. "Maybe we could go sit down?"

The three of them looked at me like I'd burped in church.

"Are you inviting yourself further into my home?" Victorine asked, with her faint, cool smile.

"I've already been in your fancy living room, your exquisite kitchen, the red bedroom where Daniel did his best not to die, the library where Daniel swore allegiance, and the basement, also known as the murder room, where you threw sharp things at me. Oh, and that conservatory upstairs. Do you even *have* secret spaces left?"

I looked around as if the crown moldings would reveal something new. Instead, a flash of movement outside the window revealed Crow perched on a wrought iron railing, silhouetted by the street-light.

A guardian of the night. Guardian of a *sleepless* night, which seemed to happen a lot when I got mixed up in these things.

"Ah, Zelda. I forget how amusing you are." She slipped her hands into her bathrobe pockets, for once almost girlish rather than ageless, and tilted her head in thought before seeming to come to a decision. "The three of you may join me in my garret." She retreated upstairs with silent steps.

"A garret?" I said, wondering what she meant. A garret seemed far too shabby for someone like Victorine.

James and Jessica had returned to glaring at each other as soon as Victorine's back was turned.

I stepped between them. "Come along, kids. Don't want to keep the Lady Victorine waiting." Then I led the way upstairs, our formation a triangle with me at the point, James and Jessica behind me, hopefully not deciding to kill each other on the way up.

Old-time photos still lined the walls in the stairwell. When we reached the next floor, we followed Victorine to another, smaller staircase that led upwards once more, to the level of an attic. Compared to Poppy's townhouse, which was a pretty simple upstairs, downstairs arrangement with two bedroom suites over a living room and kitchen, this place was a never-ending spiral of rooms upon rooms. A large crystal doorknob winked in a white door at the top of the stairs.

Victorine unlocked the door with an old-fashioned key and let us in.

23

Wooden beams framed the sharp angle of the roof. Beneath them, exposed brick walls radiated coolness. A miniature fireplace was tucked into one wall, and a skinny window into another. A built-in bookcase fit snugly next to the window, and a desk with a chair fit in the corner. A small couch and thickly cushioned armchairs filled a seating area around a colorful antique rug.

The age of the furniture wasn't far off from Prospero's Gramercy Park apartment, but the style was far more relaxed. Cheerful even. Vintage prints were displayed on every wall, and set in the bookcase, on shelves where books didn't take up the entire space.

James and Jessica hung back, but I moved closer to the prints.

First: A church surrounded by oak trees thick with moss, and several palm trees. Under the artwork, regal printed letters spelled out *Le Couvent* in small caps. Another framed piece depicted two-story buildings with large white shutters and ornate iron railings that curved around corners. A third piece showed a little alleyway with run-down charm, hung with clothing, frozen in time on laundry day. Every print was different, but seen all together, they clearly depicted the same place. "Where is this?"

"New Orleans," Victorine said, seating herself behind the desk. She gestured to the fireplace. "Will you do the honors? There is a chill in the night."

A match could do it just as well, but I liked to practice, so I knelt. Seasoned wood had already been laid, and a basket held discarded copies of the *New York Times*. I stuffed paper under the wood and did as Poppy had taught me, sending a controlled pop of fire into it. The burst of magic woke Patty Melt, who blinked sleepily in my mind before closing her eyes and going back to sleep. "What's 'Le Couvent'?"

"The convent," Victorine replied. "I grew up there."

Jessica's gaze narrowed on the art in question.

"It's not a secret," Victorine continued. "Lord Prospero and I are well aware of each other's histories. I decorated my little upstairs retreat to remind me of home."

Home. It wasn't a word I associated with Victorine. She floated through every environment like an icy angel, untouched. I looked around again, taking in the softness and the colors.

"Victorine Laguerre," Jessica said, almost to herself, as she studied the print of the convent. "*Victory in the war.* Is that your true name, Lady Victorine?"

The question walked the line between curiosity and impertinence. A lesser being than Victorine might have bristled, but the vampiress waited for Jessica to make eye contact, seeking an answer.

Then Victorine smiled, showing perfect teeth, canines beginning to sharpen. "It is *true*, Initiate. Whether it is my true name, or not."

James hid a smile as Jessica blanched.

"Now," Victorine said, stacking a sheaf of papers on her desk, "you will tell me why you believe you are becoming human."

"Yeah, how do we even know you're telling the truth?" James said.

Victorine turned her head like a hawk sighting a lizard.

James shrank back. "I'm just going to sit down, over here, and be quiet." He dropped into a plush armchair.

Jessica followed suit, oddly prim in her movement to smooth her short, pleated skirt as she sat on the edge of the couch.

"Zelda?" Victorine asked. "Are you going to stalk around or sit?"

"If I sit I'll fall asleep." The snap and crackle of the fire wasn't helping. "James is right, though. How will we know if Jessica is telling the truth?" I didn't bother to add *no offense*, to Jessica, because I didn't particularly care if she took offense.

"You may have her repeat anything you doubt, in front of your mind-reading friend," Victorine said. She turned back to Jessica. "We know the beginning of your story. You were converted at the same time as James. Placed under Lord Prospero's protection when your Elder was... removed from his position."

"From life," I corrected.

Victorine acknowledged this with a slight head bow—taking credit, not blame—before continuing. "You captured Zelda's ex-boyfriend, Daniel, a civilian, and brought him to death's door. In fact, if it hadn't been for Zelda—if Daniel had died—you would have broken the Covenant. Your own life would have been forfeit. In saving Daniel, Zelda saved *you* as well. For that, you owe her a debt that has not been paid."

Jessica owed *me*? I'd never thought about it that way before.

It may have been the shifting of the flames in the fireplace, but Victorine's expression appeared to darken. "Look at me, Initiate."

Jessica raised her head.

Even in the tender golden orange light, I could see she wasn't young at all, hadn't been for decades. Lines framed her eyes. Hair that had been so ultra-black it glowed now caught the light with tiny silver threads. Her eyes, with the red fading out like sunset, had always been older, wiser, more hardened than they should have been, for someone who looked twenty at most—but for the first time, their age matched the rest of her.

The slow snap of the fire kept time like an irregular heartbeat. Jessica took a slow breath, appeared to gather herself, before speaking. "I did as Lord Prospero said—to drink from the human—"

"From *Daniel*," I said. "Say it."

"From Daniel." Her fingers twisted together.

"Go on," Victorine said.

"I didn't think it would kill him. I thought—I thought I was close, but not quite—"

I couldn't stop myself. "You played with his *life*—you made *jokes* about it—"

"This is how I *survive*," she said. "What am I going to be, a short-order cook like him?" She jerked her head toward James.

"Better a short-order cook than a lapdog for a monster," he replied.

"Shut up, James. You did what you had to do, too."

James looked away, making me wonder just what he had done. They held each other's dark secrets like radioactive gems.

"You can judge me," Jessica said, her gaze darting to me before settling with a kind of sulky defiance on Victorine, who seemed faintly amused by it, "but I *liked* what I could do."

"You liked what you did to Daniel? Or the power you had in doing it?" I said.

"Does it matter?" she said, with a bitter laugh.

"Yes, it matters!" I marched over to her, bent down, putting my face level with hers. I half-expected Victorine to intervene, but she didn't move. "When you hurt him, I decided if I met you in a dark alley, only one of us would come out of it. Change my mind."

"How did you convince Daniel to let you stay with him? Did you appeal to his *better nature*?" Jessica said. "Or did you use what you had to get what you wanted?"

My hand came up, ready to slap her face—until I saw that it was what she wanted. To get to me. I lowered my hand. "Flirting with Daniel isn't the same as sinking your teeth into his neck." We were *not* the same. I was *not* like Jessica. I—

I *meant* well.

Jessica just looked at me. And what was left of the red in her gaze easily pierced, laser-like, the comforting fiction I told myself. I'd roped Daniel into this because I wanted a place to stay. I played on memories and desire, to get it. Simple as that. It was amazing Daniel hadn't played me right back.

Maybe he was better than I was.

Maybe I was the *real* vampire.

I turned away.

Victorine was talking now. Picking up where I couldn't continue. Asking how Jessica knew her powers were fading.

"My appearance, first," Jessica said. "Then I got tired more easily. I couldn't keep up anymore. And I started to crave... *real food*," she said, as if it still surprised her.

That got me. I almost laughed. "That part's not as bad as you think," I said, unable to stop myself from being a cheerleader of all things food-related.

"Oh, great," she said. "I'm going to die but at least there are sandwiches."

"Welcome to humanity."

She stared into the fire.

"Couldn't someone just... re-bite you?" I said. I couldn't believe I was actually troubleshooting for Jessica, of all people, but there we were.

Victorine tapped her chin thoughtfully. "The Blessed don't partake of each other—but even if we did, this condition could be catching. No one would do it of their own free will."

There was a pause. Then Victorine, Jessica, and I all looked at James.

"Bite... Jessica?" he said, hope and disgust twisting his face into a very weird expression.

"Don't touch me," Jessica said—but her expression looked just like his.

"Off topic," I said. "We'll get to that. What exactly was Prospero doing with the Mirror?"

"He doesn't tell me everything," Jessica said. "But he's been disappearing a lot, lately."

"Why were you meeting secretly with Daniel?"

Mild surprise crossed her face. "He told you?"

"Of course he did." He definitely hadn't. Not at first. But Jessica didn't need to know that.

"I mean, Prospero *was* trying to recruit him, so..."

Had Daniel mentioned that little detail? No, he had not. *Trust restored is stronger than espresso, sweeter than ice cream, and more comforting than a boat of pot roast gravy.* It better damn well be, anyway. "Why did he want to recruit someone he nearly had killed?"

"He said Daniel's new state was 'interesting.'"

James shook his head. "I wouldn't want to be 'interesting' to Lord Prospero."

"It could be to your benefit," Jessica said. "Sometimes."

In that brief exchange of normal-sounding talk, I could almost hear what they would have sounded like as friends. Before vampires and blood and a quarter of a lifetime locked in a power-based hierarchy. "And he was invited to the Royal Ball? At the Vespers Club?"

Jessica nodded. "He was coming with me. I was the go-between for him and Lord Prospero."

Well, now I knew how I was going to chat with Prospero.

Victorine spoke. "You are here and asking for help, yet you wish to return to Lord Prospero? Do you still consider yourself aligned to him?"

Jessica smoothed her skirt over her knees. Then she stood and crossed the floor with quick, neat steps, ending in front of me—

Where she dropped into a kneel, bowing her head.

What? I stepped back like a too-hot pan was spitting burning oil.

James looked as shocked as I felt.

Jessica looked up at me, a hint of the fanatic in her eyes. "This is the best way to discharge my debt," she said. "Lord Prospero will not help me. He will only discard me when he learns what has happened to me. I will be your Initiate, Zelda. No other's. And you will help me." Earnest. Desperate. Yes, fanatic. Still angling to get what she wanted by any means necessary. Same old Jessica.

And yet...

Better to snag her now than give her a chance to change her mind. Better to take away everything belonging to Prospero before he did the same to me.

I held out my hands.

Jessica took them, reverently.

"Zelda, do you accept her defection?" Victorine said.

I gazed down at Jessica. Orange fire reflected in her eyes, strength-
ening the red. She looked forged, not aged. I couldn't trust her now,
and I probably never would. But I had to admit—

I wanted her on our side.

"I accept," I said.

24

I couldn't think of a good way to break the news of Jessica's new alignment to Poppy and Aunt Belinda the next morning, so I made pancakes. Pancakes, butter, and maple syrup cover sins better than explanations. The dogs got dried liver dust and a spoonful of peanut butter mixed into their kibble, for a treat.

I served the pancakes at the tiny kitchen table, and squeezed into the third seat.

Poppy moaned happily over her fluffy stack. "You know this is my *favorite*, don't you, Zelda."

"Mm-hm," I said, swallowing a bite over a suddenly dry mouth.

"Smells real good," Aunt Belinda said, jabbing her fork through to the plate after baptizing the stack with a Niagara of real maple syrup. "Back home I usually meet my friends at McDonald's—they got free coffee for seniors—but this is a sight better-looking than the Big Breakfast."

"Thank you," I said. I let them demolish the pancakes to the half-circle point before I spoke again. "So—about last night." I cleared my throat.

Poppy's round, expressive eyes went wide with interest.

"Jessica decided not to go back to Prospero. She swore a new oath."

Aunt Belinda grunted and hacked away another forkful of pancakes.

"To me," I finished.

"Oh, my," murmured Poppy.

Aunt Belinda stopped with her fork halfway to her mouth. "Not that old-lady vampire?" asked Aunt Belinda.

"No, not Victorine," I said, picturing Victorine's face if she heard Aunt Belinda call her an old lady.

My aunt let the fork continue its flight path. She chewed thoughtfully, took a swig of coffee, set down the cup and the fork. "I ain't surprised, to be honest. That type always finds the most powerful person in the room. The trick," she said, "is to *stay* powerful. Or they'll run to someone else." She pushed back her chair and stood, then headed down the hall toward the living room.

Poppy grabbed one last bite of pancakes and followed her. Georgiana and Jester followed Poppy, both of them looking hopeful for pancake tidbits.

I stayed to clear up the plates. When I came out, Aunt Belinda stood in front of the Mirror. Her tough, wrinkled hands removed the cover we'd tied on. Her thumb grazed a carved bird's nest, and a look of pride came over her face. "My mother laid the spell on this. It's practically family." She patted the sides of the frame like you'd pat the arms of an old friend. "Speaking of family, I been talking to my Luella."

"On the phone?" I said. "Isn't that against the rules?"

"I ain't much on rules," she said, "but me and Luella, we don't need no phones. We use air magic. Like telepathy." Her expression went serious. "She's been telling me everything about the Shadows, since I ain't been in there myself. And something's just been *bothering* me." Aunt Belinda carefully touched the frame with one finger, where a gemstone dewdrop sparkled. "It ain't normal, this messing around with other dimensions. I mean, I know they exist, that's not what's getting me. It's that nobody these days has the kind of power to mess around with them. It took my mother and a whole bunch of other people just to make a single door to where the fairies live."

"Gentry," I corrected, but my heart wasn't really in it. Aunt Belinda would call them fairies out of sheer contrariness.

"Whatever," she said. "It probably took even more to put that spell around Manhattan, keeping 'em all in. Witch magic is *personal* magic. Pocket-sized magic. It takes *big* magic to do something like scrambling the pathways through dimensions, or putting whole forests full of people to sleep. Ain't nobody I know got that kind of magic. Ain't nobody I ever *heard* of got that kind of magic. Not by themselves."

I scooped up Jester, burying my face in the poufy fur on the top of his head. He smelled like oatmeal soap and dog. The Forest of Emeralds had its own perfume, too. Fallen leaves and dried moss, mineral water and dried apple chips. The memory of the golden, sleeping child beneath the apple tree squeezed my heart like a strong hand.

What magic had reached into the Forest of Emeralds and done this?

There were links. They just didn't make sense. Daniel had gone through the Forest of Emeralds to Central Park. But the flower field in Central Park led to the Arcade. The Mirror was supposed to lead to the Forest of Emeralds, but it led to the Shadows.

I was standing still, trying to think, when Jester wiggled to be put down. The instant his paws touched the floor, he fled the room.

Where was he off to? He didn't leave his people unless someone had left food, paper towels, or socks in reach.

Then Georgiana began to bark.

Was there a delivery? Jester loved to bark at deliveries. Why had he run? Why wasn't he making a sound? The last time he had gone quiet like that was—

In Daniel's apartment, the night Jessica and James had been sent to retrieve me.

A flash of heat came over me, followed by an equal amount of chill, like I was a vegetable being plunged into boiling water, then shocked by ice water to stop the cooking. Crisp-tender Zelda.

"Listen," Aunt Belinda said.

"I know, I hear the dog—"

"No, *listen*."

I held very still, straining to hear whatever it was.

And then, I heard it. Under the ringing barks, a shushing, not unlike summer rain on the roof of my old house in Florida. "Rain?"

"Wait a minute," Poppy said, moving to the window and pulling the curtain aside. "That's not rain. It's *magic*."

So much silver light billowed outside the windows it almost looked like we were underwater. The magic spun in whirlwinds, splitting and combining, waving like sheets shaken out. It wasn't water, or fabric. It was *fire*. An entire force field of magical fire, surrounding the townhouse.

The three of us stared at the silver flames outside the window.

"Some security system you got here," Aunt Belinda said.

"Wow," Poppy said. "I never knew what it would look like. It's never gone off before."

From down the hall, I heard a peep, like a tiny whistle.

Jester was peeking out from the kitchen.

"It's okay, boy," I said. I went to him, scooped him up, and kissed the soft pouf on his head again as I carried him into the living room. "Mama will keep you safe." I gently lowered him next to Georgiana, who had stopped barking and settled for grumbling suspiciously out the window.

Jester went on two legs to look out, propping his front paws on the windowsill, pretending to be a very brave boy.

I held out my hands to Poppy and Aunt Belinda. "Recharge me. I'm going outside."

"Are you sure?" Poppy said. "Is it safe?"

"Probably not. But I want to know who's out there." They took my hands. Poppy's fire magic bloomed like lace over my hand and wrist. Aunt Belinda's air magic was like my brother's, icy cold and tingling. "Thank you," I said. I went to the front door and placed my hand on the knob.

Then I took a deep breath and pulled the door open.

The wall of silver fire dissipated like mist. The usual morning bustle filled the street in both directions: cabs and trucks, pedestrians and dogs. Nothing unusual. The threat, whatever it was, was gone. I was about to step down into the street in hopes of a better view when my foot landed on something flat that made a soft crunch. I lifted my Doc Marten.

An envelope. Cream-colored. With a red wax seal on it that I had just crushed underfoot.

"What is it?" Poppy said.

"A love letter." I scooped up the envelope, found my name on the front in beautiful cursive. The pieces of wax crumbled and fell away. I swept them aside with my foot, then stepped back and shut the door.

I should have opened the envelope right away, but my hand trembled.

Poppy approached and carefully took the envelope. She brushed away the last specks of hardened red wax, lifted the flap, and withdrew a paper.

I reached out, closing my fingers on the paper before she could begin to read. "It's all right, Poppy," I said. "I can do it."

She nodded, patted me on the arm, and stepped back.

I read it.

Dear Friend,

Once upon a time, I took something that belonged to you. Now you have taken something that belongs to me. Turnabout is fair play, my friend—but I excel at games. I will have what is mine.

Yours, etc.,

Lord Prospero

I stared at the page. It might as well have been a clock, attached to a bomb.

Prospero was coming.

25

Poppy tiptoed closer and looked over my shoulder.

Aunt Belinda did the same. "'Dear *Friend*,'" she said. She made a face. "What a weirdo."

"'Weirdo' is right," Poppy said. "Also, 'psychopath.' And 'mon ster.'"

The words skittered past like water droplets on a burning hot griddle. Too many thoughts in my head. Dimensions. Mirrors. Spells. I had to face Prospero at the Royal Ball—as *Jessica*—and I had no idea what he was up to.

I closed my eyes, and all I could see was apple trees lit by golden lightning.

Dimensions. Mirrors. Spells.

Then my phone buzzed. I retrieved it, looked at the screen.

Berron?

He was notoriously bad with his phone. He either left it off, or—worse—just *left it* somewhere. He went through more cheapie

210

phones than I went through bread slices. He rarely, if ever, texted. *Where are you?* he said.

Home. Why? I wrote back.

Need to talk to you. A long pause. Then: *Also, I think I'm drunk.*

"Oh, for God's sake," I said. Berron didn't drink anything but coffee. What was he doing? I typed furiously: *Where are you?*

Another pause. I imagined him taking another swig of whatever he was drinking. Finally, a text: *Flatiron Saloon.*

I shoved my phone in my back pocket. "Berron has apparently decided that now is a good time to start drinking. He's in some Midtown joint. I'm going to get him."

"That sounds threatening," Poppy said.

"He has no idea." I'd sobered up quite a few people in my time, usually kitchen employees who showed up three sheets to the wind when we were all hands on deck for Sunday brunch. "Are you sure you'll be okay here?"

Aunt Belinda grinned. "I ain't got my pistol, but me and Miss Poppy got all the magic we need between us."

"Quite right," Poppy said. "And a lovely fiery security system, too. And the best watchdogs on the Upper West Side!"

"True," I said, giving Jester one more scritchy-scratch before I left. "Be good, boy." He licked my hand. I fed him a slightly fuzzy dried liver treat from my pocket.

Then I left.

I walked to a busier corner and hailed a cab. Couldn't waste time walking. Couldn't risk Berron changing his mind and slipping out of the Flatiron Saloon, disappearing into the streets of Midtown, holing up in some tiny forgotten park to gaze, pickled, at a tree.

Damn it. It wasn't like him. He drank coffee almost compulsively. Espresso, drip, cold brew, French press, you name it. But not alcohol.

The cab stopped. A trellis framed the restaurant entrance, wreathed with vines so old and thick they looked like knotted ropes. Warm light glowed inside.

I pushed open the door and entered.

It wasn't a dive, I'd give it that. Berron had picked a classy joint to get drunk. Wood cabinets filled with bottles lined the walls. Each cabinet was lit from the inside, making the bottles sparkle. Two-tops took up the floor, and a long banquette ran down one wall, parallel to a bar along the other wall. A mirror and more bottles behind the bar. The far end of the room was taken up by a small stage hung with velvet curtains. The air smelled like whiskey and bar snacks and Midtown finance guy cologne.

Someone was making their way onto the stage. An acoustic guitarist, I thought. Only when he took the steps, he wasn't holding a guitar—he was holding the railing. Unsteadily. Unfolding. His height increasing with each step. Longish dark hair hanging forward over his face—

"Oh, no," I said.

The Prince of the Gentry was taking the stage.

He slid his fingers through his hair, sweeping the long tresses back, revealing eyes bright with stage lights and alcohol. "This is a song," he said, pausing to search the audience until his gaze landed on me, "dedicated to my Zelda."

I cupped my hands around my mouth. "Not your Zelda!"

He blew me a kiss, then closed his eyes and gripped the microphone on its stand. His baritone voice hummed with resonance that made the ordinary fade away. The room got darker and starrier at the same time, and I swore I heard the shrill harmony of crickets.

Berron's words, when he sang, were these:

Over hill, over dale, through bush, through brier,

Over park, over pale, through flood, through fire

I do wander everywhere, swifter than the moon's sphere;

And I serve the Fairy Queen, to dew her orbs upon the green;

The cowslips tall her pensioners be; in their gold coats spots you see;

Those be rubies, fairy favours; in those freckles live their savours;

I must go seek some dewdrops here, and hang a pearl in every

cowslip's ear.

Something pulsed under my boots as he sang. I lifted one foot. Beneath it, tendrils of vines pushed up from beneath the floorboards, growing tiny leaves and flowers.

The audience that hadn't even looked up when he spoke or I shouted, stared rapt as he finished the song, only seeming to wake as the resonance faded away. They shook their heads, as if dazed, and then returned to their own conversations as if they'd already forgotten the song.

Berron swayed, and released the microphone. Caught my gaze again. Judging by his unsteadiness, there was a real chance he might fall off the stage and lie on the floor, smelling the fairy flowers and the floorboards until he passed into unconsciousness.

I hurried forward, took the stage steps in one jump, and slid an arm around him.

He draped his arm casually around my shoulder, as if this was something we did every day, something completely normal. "Zelda," he said, "you came. Did you like my song?"

"Great song, Berron. I love it when people get drunk and sing at me. In public. While conjuring plants out of the floor."

He blinked, dipped his head closer to my ear with the air of someone wise sharing a secret. "You're being sarcastic."

"You think?"

"Mmm."

There was a vacant booth at the corner of the stage, a private one, and I managed to steer His Royal Drunkenness into it. "Stay here. Try not to fall over. I'm going to get you a coffee."

"I serve the Fairy Queen," he said, before putting his head down on the table with a *thunk*.

I hustled to the bar and ordered a double shot, returning to the alcove with several ounces of pure rocket fuel. "Drink," I said, setting the espresso down and scooting into the booth next to Berron.

Berron hauled himself upright. His hair shifted, revealing pointed ears.

"Berron! You're supposed to be disguising yourself, not showing off your Gentry ears to anyone who happens to look." I seized several locks of hair and tried to arrange them over his ears.

"You care," he said. He closed his eyes and tilted his head back. The smile of a saint and a sinner rolled into one, lips the color of rose petals.

"Fix your ears. Drink." I shook him, not gently, until he sat up straight and opened his eyes. Then I pressed the cup into his hand.

He regarded it dubiously, then threw it back in one gulp. He put it down and smoothed his hair; when he took his hands away, the lobes of his ears were round again. "Happy?"

"Yeah, can't you tell?"

He looked at me. "Do 'murder eyes' mean you're happy?"

"I can't believe you're not taking this seriously. I mean, this is *your realm* that's in trouble. And you're off in some Midtown bar, getting trashed? What about that golden child you showed me under the apple tree?"

Berron made a soft sound, like I'd said something amusing.

"What's funny?"

"'Golden child.' She is, you know. She always was." He paused. "That's what I had to tell you."

"What are you talking about?"

"My sister." The clink of glasses and flatware faded out as if stifled, replaced by the whisper of wind in the highest of trees, the soft thump of an apple falling from its branch.

That sleeping Gentry girl curled up at the base of an apple tree?

His *sister*?

Berron's sister?

It was on the tip of my tongue to say: *Why didn't you tell me?*

Instead I held still, hoping that if I disappeared, he would keep talking instead of bolting back into the forest of his secrets.

"It should have been me," he said. "She is the Princess of Arrows. She was born to lead. She was always more clever than me." He shook his head. "The number of times I tried to wake her, only to watch her fall asleep again..."

"You can't lose hope—"

He seized my hands, folded them in his own and drew them to his heart. "I will make you my Queen. I swear. Only do this for me. Free my sister. Free my people. Let them live again."

"Berron, you don't need to—"

"I'll make sandwiches for you. Forever. You won't have to pay me."

I extricated my hands from his. "Berron. You great, hulking idiot. You think you have to"—I paused, looking for the right word—"*woo* me to get me to help. You don't. I would help you if you were a two-foot-tall talking lizard named Moe, and your lizard people were trapped in the dying Lizard Realm."

He stared at me. "You don't understand."

"I don't understand what?"

"The fact that you would help Moe the Lizard Man without a second thought is why I—" He stopped. He moved closer. His hand, his long fingers, caressed my cheek. "I would give you everything."

I knew the kiss was coming. I could have turned away. Happy-ever-afters are for suckers. *Forever* is just a word that sells greeting cards.

And yet I let it happen.

Slowly. Reverently. The touch of his lips on my lower lip alone, as if he knew I would bolt if he moved too fast. The bitterness of fresh coffee. Magic spinning between us like leaves in a whirlwind. The scent of cut apples in the air, as if we weren't deep in a concrete canyon but free, in an orchard, without a care.

His kiss wrapped me in a fantasy I didn't believe in.

Why did it have to taste so good?

26

J ester lifted his head from where he was curled in the blue velvet side chair by the bedroom window, alert for voices floating up from the living room.

"They're here, buddy." I straightened the bed pillows. I hadn't pulled down the vines Berron magicked onto the walls yet, even though they were beginning to wilt. The vines would have to stay for now. "It's time," I said.

He jumped down and trotted across the room, to the closed door, where he turned and gave me a look.

"You don't have to go out," I said. "They'll come to us."

And within a minute, the sound of footsteps on the stairs. A knock at the door. Then Poppy's voice: "Hello! Everyone's here!"

"Are you decent?" called Aunt Belinda.

I was wearing my Peaseblossom outfit. It was comfortable, and it felt right. I opened the door.

There they were: Victorine, Poppy, Aunt Belinda, and Jessica.

"Ugh, thank God you're decent," Jessica said. "Lady Zelda," she added, dropping a quick curtsy. How can a curtsy be sarcastic?

218

Maybe it was just brief because she had her hands full. She was hauling a garment bag big enough for a wedding dress, and a smaller bag like a soft-sided hatbox.

Victorine glided in. Poppy practically galloped inside. Aunt Belinda came next, followed by Jessica with her bags. I peeked into the hallway. "Georgiana?"

"Downstairs," Poppy said. "Keeping your prom date company."

"Daniel is not my prom date," I said, shutting the door.

"He is, though," she said.

Jessica was busy unzipping the garment bag. A white dress covered in gold embroidery spilled out, followed by a thick red velvet train. She shook the dress out and laid it flat.

Jester went on two legs, the better to see the clothing on the bed. I could see he was thinking about how delicious and chewy it would be. Nothing Jester liked better than a big mouthful of clothes. I moved the edges of the dress out of reach.

Jessica unzipped the hatbox and flipped the lid open. She withdrew a wildly sparkling crown with hundreds of faceted crystals and tiny white pearls, and a matching hair comb.

Victorine examined the costume. "Replicas of the coronation dress and the crown of Empress Josephine, are they not?"

"Yes," Jessica said. "Lady Victorine." The title was more respectful aimed at Victorine, but with just enough of a delay to make you wonder *how* respectful.

Victorine acted like she hadn't heard. Instead, she idly traced the filigree on the crown. "Were you thinking Lord Prospero would crown you tonight?"

If Jessica had been a pressure cooker, steam would have leaked from her ears.

"It's a beautiful costume," I said, hoping the compliment would distract her from starting an ill-advised brawl with Victorine.

"Oh, yes," Poppy echoed. "Beautiful."

"Right pretty," Aunt Belinda said.

Thank goodness they picked up on cues.

Jessica relaxed, ever so slightly. "I like the painting," she said. "Of the coronation." It was the first time Jessica had offered an opinion on anything that wasn't mayhem-related. A miracle, really.

I scooped up the dress and held it against myself. Too small by a long shot. Jessica was both shorter and more petite than I'd ever be. But I didn't need to wear it—I only needed to examine it closely and let the mask do the work of creating a perfect duplicate.

Jester sniffed around the hem, trying to determine if this exciting-smelling new thing was part of me, and therefore off-limits for biting. He snuck in a few tiny kisses before I took it out of his reach by laying it face-down on the bed, the better to see the back of it.

I was pretty sure I had it. But I ran my hands over the dress one more time, the better to feel the texture of the velvet, the fur trim, the fine white fabric.

Then I was ready.

I touched my fingers to my temples, conscious of the glittering diamond mask that was always there, but invisible to everyone else. Excitement built even before the magic activated. I concentrated on the dress: white gown, satin, empire waist, with gold trim and embroidered golden bees; rose-red velvet train embellished with gold and lined with ermine. I closed my eyes and summoned the disguising magic.

Pinpoints of starry diamonds exploded around me. For a moment, a feeling of weightlessness, like I might float away and bump my head into the ceiling, before gravity called me home again. The glittering diamonds flashed rainbows all around me before fading away.

I opened my eyes and looked down at myself. From my point of view, my costume floated, ghostlike, over my real clothes. When I looked in the mirror I could see the full effect: a dress fit for a Royal Ball.

Jester returned to sniffing curiously at my feet, as if I'd done something interesting but he couldn't quite figure out what it was, or if he could possibly bite it.

"What do you think, boy?"

He sneezed.

"Fancy!" Aunt Belinda said. "Now do the rest."

"The important part," Poppy said. "The *crown*." She had it in her hands, turning it over and over, wide-eyed and splashed with glimmers of light. She placed the crown on her own head and did the royal wave. "Hello! I'm Queen Poppy!"

"I think *I'm* the important part, actually," Jessica said.

"She's right," I said. "The costume is a costume. But I can't go to the Ball as Zelda. Jessica—closer, please." I needed a good look at her. The curves of her face, the arch of her eyebrows, right down to the insolent set of her mouth and the tiny new wrinkles blooming at the corners. Just like studying those old magazine pictures, only in 3D.

"Hands," I said. She held them out. For someone so committed to destruction, they were surprisingly delicate. The lines circling her knuckles were a clue to her real age but also a hint to her toughness. I stepped back. "Turn, please."

She rotated, slowly.

"Okay." Everyone was staring at me, except for Jester, who seemed to think Jessica might do something interesting after spinning around. Stage fright fluttered through my stomach. Fancy dresses were easy in comparison. I turned away, the better to concentrate.

Jessica. Young vampiress turning middle-aged. Shorter than me, smaller than me, a compact gothic terror in red lipstick. I had to *be* her, without a doubt, without a suspicion, to fool her former Elder. I'd done this on the fly before—turning into a fake Victorine, or following Daniel incognito—but I *really* couldn't afford an error now.

The disguise would have to pass inspection with *everyone* before I trusted it to work on Prospero.

I held the image of Jessica in my mind and activated the mask magic once more. The flickering rainbow pinpoints did their work, spilling over me like a waterfall of diamond dust.

When they subsided, I turned back to my audience. "Well?"

Jester, taking this as a cue, immediately sat down and looked up at me for a treat.

"Not you, boy. I was asking them."

He tilted his head, and his tongue lolled out with happy incomprehension.

Aunt Belinda was the first to approach. She looked back and forth between Jessica and me. "Don't that beat all," she said. "What do you all think?"

"I think Jessica is the one who sees that face in the mirror every day," Victorine said. "What she thinks is paramount."

All eyes turned to Jessica. She said nothing at first, only stared at me with an unreadable expression, which I interpreted as *You look nothing like me* and *Start over, it stinks.*

Then she spoke.

"You need the crown."

Poppy hastily pulled it off her own head and placed it on mine. Jessica wordlessly passed her the matching hair comb, which Poppy carefully tucked into my hair. "Empress Zelda," she said. She dropped a deep curtsy, one of those old-fashioned sweeping ones, before stepping back.

Jessica eyed me critically for a long moment. "Stop looming," she said.

"Excuse me?" I said.

"You loom. I don't."

"She *insinuates*," Poppy said.

I made a face. "What does that even look like?"

"Like this." Jessica walked across the room, and now that I was looking for it, I could see the difference. She was the slinky model of nineties fashion magazines: all dark eyeliner, angles, and boredom.

"I can 'insinuate,'" I said. I'd changed my posture before, just not like this. As a chef I always folded up a little when talking to an unhappy customer; it made them less aggressive. When I flirted I let my curves do the talking. This couldn't be any worse.

I crossed my bedroom, faithfully imitating Jessica's walk. Then I leaned against the wall as if the *Vogue* photographer might snap my picture at any moment. "See?"

No one applauded.

"I can do it," Aunt Belinda said. She put her hands on her hips and crossed the room like a flamingo.

"That might have been an improvement," Jessica said.

I stuck my tongue out at her.

"It will do," Victorine said.

Poppy clapped her hands briskly. "Come along, everyone," she said. "Zelda needs her power-up." She shepherded Victorine, Jessica, and Aunt Belinda toward me.

"Not me," Jessica said. "I'll mess it up."

"You, too," I said, in a voice that didn't allow argument. Maybe she was weaker than she had been. Maybe she couldn't contribute much. But I needed everything I could get.

Victorine's cool hand lay on my left shoulder, Aunt Belinda's strong one on my right. I flashed back to melting the Mirror ice as Poppy took my right hand, and Jessica my left. Then I just had to let all of it hit me, like opening an oven door and a reach-in fridge, or standing in front of an air conditioning vent and a hot subway tunnel all at once. Blown over and blasted. Magic that singed, magic that froze, magic that burned, spiraling around and through me until I felt as overstuffed as a pastrami sandwich.

"I'm good," I managed to say.

They withdrew, Aunt Belinda with one last pat on the back.

I breathed deeply, shook out my hands. "Let's do this." I was about to open the door and sweep down the stairs when Aunt Belinda gave me a look indicating she had something to say. "We'll be right down," I said to Victorine, Poppy, and Jessica.

They went out, leaving Aunt Belinda, Jester, and me.

Jester peered back and forth between us.

"I'm sending Crow with you," Aunt Belinda said, "because I don't see how you're going to carry or use your phone in that get-up."

I looked down at the elaborate illusion. "Yeah, I'd give myself away."

Aunt Belinda nodded. "Something goes wrong, you tell Crow. What he knows, I know. And I can use my phone, and so can your friends."

"What if you need to tell *me* something?"

"My air magic lets me talk telepathically. Like I do with Luella. You'll hear me in your ear, if it comes to that." She patted me on the shoulder, then appeared to reconsider, and threw her arms around me, squeezing me to the point of bones cracking before pulling back. "You be careful out there, you hear?"

"I will. Get in, get out, go have a late-night snack."

She patted my cheek.

We left the bedroom. My ghostly train slid down the stairs behind me, both *there* and *not there*. Real enough to feel its weight; magic enough to feel as if it floated.

Jester shot ahead, scrabbling down the stairs at full speed, then launching himself onto the couch and into Daniel's lap.

"Jester! Hey, boy!" With lots of firm pats, he managed to get Jester to settle next to him rather than climb onto his head. Jester's tail pouf whipped back and forth in pure excitement.

Daniel stood.

His outfit was the same as he had worn into the Forest of Emeralds: inky black shirt; slacks, vest, and jacket subtly patterned with cobweb white. When he adjusted the jacket, the red lining flashed like satin blood. The new addition to his outfit was a dark red rose boutonniere—and Prospero's cane, leaning against the couch. "Zelda Hawkins," he said. "You look... like Jessica."

This wasn't right. I would have to spend the whole night as someone else. For now, I wanted him to see me as me. I activated the mask again, keeping the costume, but letting Jessica's appearance fade away.

"Let me rephrase that," Daniel said, when the transformation was complete. "You look—stunning." He picked up a white box from the coffee table and held it out.

I took it, pulled at the elaborate gold ribbon until it fell.

Jester dove off the couch and snatched it up in his jaws.

"I'll get it," Poppy said, reaching for a dog treat to trade for the ribbon.

I opened the box. Inside, a single oversized red rose rested, surrounded by tiny yellow and purple flowers.

"It was really hard to find those," Daniel said. "But I finally found a florist who special-ordered them."

I touched the velvety petals.

"You recognize them?"

I shook my head, then dipped my nose into the box. Rose, of course, but also hints of orange, vanilla, and honey.

"Peaseblossom and mustardseed," he said. "And look underneath."

I lifted the corsage from the box, set the box down, and then eased the largest rose petals aside so I could see the base of the corsage. A swatch of Daniel's cobweb fabric cradled the flowers—and a miniature silver moth had been pinned to the fabric. "Oh, Daniel. It's gorgeous."

"Let me help you." He took the corsage and placed it on my shoulder, where the train met the dress, using safety pins he pulled from his pocket to make it secure. "There."

I hugged him with care, so as not to crush the gift. His cologne mingled with the scents of the flowers.

He stepped back, cleared his throat, then gestured at me. "Go ahead. Do your thing."

I didn't want to. Becoming Jessica put up a wall between us; he wouldn't be the same Daniel, the one who brought me flowers and let me embrace him. I picked up Jester—who still had one of those alfalfa chews in his mouth—and buried my face in his fur. My best beloved. "Wish me luck, boy," I said. When I put him down, I had those funny sparkles all over me.

It was time to transform.

Some days, you get up and cook egg sandwiches.

Other days, you crash a vampire ball.

27

We snuck out the back, using the tiny patio off my bedroom to reach the fire escape, in case the front of the house was being watched by any of Prospero's minions. The night wind rose, whipping away the scent of the flowers and replacing it with a less-sweet combination of exhaust and evening meals. Daniel tucked Prospero's cane under his arm and held his hands out for me to take the last step from fire escape to solid ground.

It was hard enough to manage all the magic sloshing around, let alone remember to *insinuate*, like Jessica showed me. We made our way down a tiny alley and reached the parallel street to the north of the townhouse.

Poppy and Victorine would leave separately, and be in the vicinity of the Royal Ball. Just in case. Aunt Belinda was staying behind to watch the townhouse, the dogs, and Jessica. No good having a doppelganger show up when you're trying to be someone you're not. James and Lily were holding down the evening shift at the shop, and although playing dress-up was fun, an apron and a ponytail sounded a lot more relaxing than this.

And Berron...

Berron had promised to stay out of it, because he was the only being left with Gentry magic, and I needed him.

Because of his magic, obviously.

But I had to assume he wouldn't be too far away. He couldn't *not* be involved—it wasn't in his nature.

Unlike the first Vespers Club I'd crashed, in the Lower East Side, this one was closer to my own turf. Upper East Side. Almost straight across Central Park, not too far from Victorine's. Another abandoned church—or, more accurately, a sold-out church. The diocese had ignored the pleas of the congregation in favor of a fat check from a developer. And so the church, which had been named for a Hungarian saint pictured with arms full of bread and roses, sat forsaken.

We took a cab, choosing to arrive a block away and approach on foot. The walk would give everyone else time to get in place. I looped the velvet train over my arm and silently thanked the magic for allowing me to wear my own comfortable Doc Martens while appearing to wear white slippers.

Daniel had barely spoken since we left, seeming to clam up around "Jessica," but as we walked, he piped up again. "I looked up the church."

"Yeah, I saw it was bought out by a developer."

"Did you see who used to go there?"

I shook my head, thinking he was about to name one of New York's many celebrity residents.

"It was the only Catholic congregation for the deaf in the city."

"And they shut it down?"

"There was a whole thing in the *Times* about it." Daniel, for all his polish and worldliness, hid a moral streak that ran deep in unexpected places.

I wasn't religious, myself, but even I could be moved by devotion. Community. Having a place to belong. Apparently, when Daniel and I found common ground, it had to be formerly consecrated.

"I think this is it," he said, gesturing to a building with a dozen gracefully arched windows in a brownstone facing. Crosses topped a green copper spire and two more decorative copper roof finishings. The main entrance consisted of four large red doors with gold kickplates, set beneath a matching red archway with a stained glass trefoil. The doorway seemed strangely oversized, a portal out of sync with the rest of the street's more modest entrances.

This gathering wasn't open to witches. There was a strict guest list of the Blessed who were permitted to attend. Victorine and James weren't on it. Daniel and "Jessica" were. I put my free arm through Daniel's and we walked up to the red doors.

Daniel knocked.

The door cracked open. A Blessed I didn't know blocked the way. She saw Daniel first, made a skeptical face—

Then she saw me. "Jessica! Right this way. Lord Prospero has been asking for you."

Insinuate, I thought. "This is Daniel," I said, with that special mix of boredom, flirtation, and venom Jessica did so well. "He's on the list."

"Of course." The Blessed backed away.

I let my train fall. It swept behind me as we passed through the doorway.

The entrance had me fooled. From the outside, it looked like the doors would open directly into the sanctuary itself. Instead, we entered an empty, pitch-black foyer facing a steep set of stairs. Daniel and I shared a brief look—*Are you ready?* it said—before climbing.

At the top of the stairs, a second set of doors, unguarded. Daniel stepped forward and pushed one open.

Inside, light bloomed. *Everything* bloomed. There were roses everywhere: garlands of red and white roses, scattered pink rose petals, all over a row of pews so simple and earnest that I wanted to pet one like it was a lost puppy. Only the ceiling laid claim to being truly grand. Stone vaults framed a ceiling painted midnight blue and covered with eight-pointed gold stars. At the corners of the vaults, solemn, haloed angels in white robes held harps and gazed down. Probably wondering where the previous congregation had gone.

There was no witchy bartender this time. No colorful punk band. Only the silky hum of a crowd of the Blessed in every kind of velvet and satin, crown and mask, and a Blessed string quartet playing a waltz in the front corner of the sanctuary. Candelabras threw orange light and shifting shadows over everything.

To the side of the pews, a statue of a woman with her arms full of baguettes and roses. I couldn't decide if it was more or less respectful to copy a saint's motif for party decorations. Then a flutter of black descended from the night sky ceiling and landed, with a balancing wingbeat, on the statue's head.

Crow—come to watch, and thankfully invisible to anyone without elemental magic.

We walked down the aisle, crushing petals underfoot. Was my walk more like Aunt Belinda's or Jessica's? Too late to turn back now.

Prospero—*Lord* Prospero, if I was Jessica—waited. His deep black cape almost blotted out the ornate chair on which he sat. Beneath the cape, he wore a formal outfit straight out of Victorian times: tailored slacks of dark fabric; a navy sash crossing a pure white dress shirt; and, as decoration, a thick scarlet ribbon holding a gold medal suspended over his heart. If he *had* a heart left, and not a bag of dust.

Only a few short steps upward separated us from the dais where he sat. I dipped my head, curtsied exactly as Jessica had shown me. "My Lord," I murmured.

"Jessica," he said, a fond professor chastising his favorite student. "You picked a strange time to go on one of your jaunts."

Eyes still down, worshipful at the feet of my superior. "I wanted to look perfect tonight, my Lord."

"And so you do. I see you have brought our old acquaintance."

I raised my head at last, to look at Daniel. Placing one hand on his shoulder, as if to give him permission. "As my Lord commands."

Daniel held out Prospero's cane with both hands. "I believe this belongs to you, sir."

Prospero regarded him. "Why, indeed it does. How thoughtful." He almost smiled, as if at a private joke, when he took the cane. "There are many in need of a waltzing partner this evening, my friend," Prospero said. "Why not avail yourself? Return to me later, and we shall talk."

Daniel, dismissed, glanced at me once more before fading into the crowd.

I climbed the steps, mindful not to clomp or loom, and took my place beside Prospero's makeshift throne.

"I have been thinking about young Daniel," he said, resting the cane, scepter-like, across his body.

"My Lord?"

"Despite our... rocky beginning, as it were, I believe he has fair prospects."

"Prospects?"

"Wealth. Access. A sort of worldly ease that could allow him to move seamlessly between the society of the Blessed and that of the less gifted."

I said nothing, figuring that was the safest bet.

"I should like to bring him into our set," Prospero continued. "He belongs with us, not with the riffraff with whom he currently associates."

We watched the dancers whirl across the floor in the open space between the front pews and the dais. Daniel's pent-up energy had been flung into spinning a lady of the Blessed possibly a little harder than she bargained for, judging by the expression on her face.

"What say you, Jessica?" A generous monarch allowing an opinion.

The obvious answer: to agree with everything. "He would make a fine Initiate," I said.

Prospero nodded, absently, as if my answer was acceptable but not quite correct. "After tonight, the Blessed will begin a new life." Certainty in his dark eyes. "I am sure you are curious."

I let Jessica's teasing side come out. "Of course, my Lord."

"Never fear, child. All shall be revealed."

It was all I could do not to slap him across his perfectly calm face. Not only was he not going to tell me—Jessica—what was going on, he was going to do something *tonight*. This had been an intelligence-gathering mission only. Get in, get out, go have a late-night snack.

Not anymore.

And my only connection to the rest of the crew was a crow, sitting on a saint.

28

The ball dragged on. Lord Prospero seemed content to sit on the dais in place of a priest, watching his unholy flock amuse themselves with dancing, flirting, climbing over the pews, and taking selfies with the saint statue.

Aunt Belinda must have gotten an eyeful.

As the night aged, the fun turned shrill. Glowing vampire eyes lit with a desperation for more than kicks. Like the look on my own face after pulling a double at the restaurant without even having time to put food in my own face.

Hunger.

The Blessed didn't do catering. Unlike the Vespers Club I'd attended before, there were no willing witches to provide a snack. Maybe a few of the Blessed had brought their own vials, but I didn't see a single one sneaking a nip.

From the look on Prospero's face, he took a quiet satisfaction in watching this spirit rise. He glanced at me. "Something the matter, Initiate? You scowl. Did you not wish to dance?"

"No, my Lord." I debated whether to push further, not wanting to do anything uncharacteristic. "The mood changes. That is all."

"Ah," he said. "You disappeared before word got around. I asked that they fast before the Ball."

It took everything I had not to react visibly and audibly to this news. An abandoned church full of starving vampires. And the only viable food source in the building?

Me.

I took my train over my arm again. "I think I *will* dance, my Lord. If you will excuse me?"

He nodded regally.

I stepped down from the dais and beelined for Daniel, who had taken a break and was leaning against the wall. I put on one of Jessica's seductive smiles, to make my approach look believable to any observer. "We need to talk," I said. I took his arm and led him to the dance floor.

Waltzing wasn't my top skill. Roasting? Grilling? Knife work? I'm your gal. But my dance moves are more in the range of thrashing enthusiastically. Add to that the need to *insinuate* around the dance floor and it was enough to make me want to walk right out those big red front doors.

Whether Daniel could read that on me or not, he wrapped one arm around my waist with a strength that gave me courage. I placed my gloved hand in his, and off we went into the swaying mass of fasting vampires. At least it was a Viennese waltz, which allowed us to get close enough to speak quietly.

"He's planning something at the end of the party," I said, as close to Daniel's ear as possible. "And he's told everyone not to eat."

"I know," Daniel said. "Some of them already told me about the fasting. They think they're saving their appetites for something special."

"Did anyone say what he was planning?"

"I don't think anyone knows."

The clock was ticking. "I need you to go lean against the wall some more, by the statue of the saint. The one with bread and roses."

"St. Elizabeth."

"That's the one. Aunt Belinda's familiar is perched on it; tell the bird what's going on, and he'll pass it on. But don't let anyone see what you're doing."

"Got it."

"Now smile and look flirted with."

He complied. It would have been charming if it weren't distracting. I couldn't afford to be distracted.

I was still distracted.

"I have to get back to the altar," I said.

"Finish the dance."

I did. Although it was less of a dance and more of the two of us embracing, without seeming to; blocking out enemies and fear to hold each other; to take comfort, just the two of us, in a space once sacred. When the music stopped, I squeezed his hands. Curtsied. And left him, to return to the altar where Prospero waited.

He pulled a pocket watch from his vest. The gold cover flashed as he flicked it open. "Almost time."

How far would Jessica go? She was a demanding little thing, that was for sure. But how demanding? Knowing her place, for sure, but also dying to know what the rest of the Blessed *didn't* know. "Can you give me a hint, my Lord? Is the surprise... here?"

He chuckled, seeming to enjoy Jessica's curiosity. That scared me more than anything I'd seen so far, because the only times I had ever seen Prospero happy were times where something was about to go wrong. "Soon, pet."

Pet. I'd pet him with a knuckle sandwich. How did Jessica put up with this?

Daniel was across the room, next to the statue, not making eye contact with me. Hopefully muttering information to Crow—and by extension, Aunt Belinda.

The Blessed looked worse for wear. They could only fast for so long, and some of them had clearly pushed past their endurance. Several sprawled in the pews. Their royal robes and skirts dragged the floor.

Prospero observed without comment.

Finally, a nervous trio approached the altar. "Lord Prospero," one of them said, who was dressed like Henry the Eighth but had a face like a fox. "We beg your indulgence, my Lord. May we inquire when we might break this... fast?"

Prospero was too refined to smirk. Instead, he gazed into the distance, as if the answer might be found through the darkened stained glass windows facing the street. "I believe," he said, mildly, "that to 'break fast' is traditionally done at sunrise." He returned his gaze to the fox-faced man. "Is it not?"

"Yes, my Lord. Absolutely. My apologies." He bowed his way backwards, taking his companions with him.

Prospero watched them go. "You see, Jessica," he said, "a leader must know when to wield the thorns, and when to wield the petals."

"Yes, my Lord."

"You may wonder why I am telling you this."

Because you like to hear the sound of your own voice? I thought. But I arched my eyebrows instead, to show my attention as Jessica would.

"You will learn to recognize greatness this way."

"Why should I need to recognize any greatness but yours, my Lord?"

He said nothing. And then he laid his hand on my gloved one, and patted my hand.

I froze. I had never gotten the impression that Prospero was a touchy-feely boss. Even Jessica would have been shocked. Was he—

Was he being *sentimental*?

He removed his hand, and cleared his throat as if he, too, had found it awkward. But necessary.

I had no clue what Jessica would have done. I stood there, trying to process the unexpected gesture of affection. You don't think of your enemy as having feelings. Not feelings that matter, anyway—in comparison to the havoc they cause, feelings are distractions. Of course he cared for Jessica, in the way that a chef cares for her best knife. But if it breaks, you get another one.

It sounded convincing. Less so when I felt the lingering warmth on my glove.

Prospero... cared?

At long last, he stood. It was all the signal the Blessed needed to stop in their tracks and turn, as one, to face the altar. "My friends," he said. "The time has come." A few of the Blessed clapped uncertainly. Prospero waited for the noise to stop before he continued. "For much of our lives we have been confined to this island. For much of mine, I have labored to discover a way out." The Blessed in the audience looked at each other.

Daniel crossed his arms.

"Today the spell falls." A rose petal could have drifted to the floor and I would have heard it. "I go this morn to open the way. I will not—" He stopped, seemingly overcome by some emotion. "I will not be returning to you." Gasps and murmurs in the crowd; he held his hand out for quiet. "Let my sacrifice not be in vain, dear ones. Go to the bridges. Prepare yourself. The spell will fall, and you must be gone. Gone before the witches realize what has happened." He almost smiled. His eyes shone. "Go into the world. Be free. If I cannot go with you, I cheer you on—in spirit." He paused. "I leave behind my best beloved to govern those who remain: Jessica, who has been my right arm these many years; and Daniel, who I have chosen as my successor. He shall henceforth be known as Lord Daniel."

My mouth dropped open. *Lord Daniel?*

The crowd turned and parted. Daniel stood in the gap, his gaze only briefly slipping to me before returning to Prospero. What a poker face Daniel had. Anyone else would have stammered and shook. You'd have thought he'd been preparing for this moment.

Prospero held out his hand. "Lord Daniel, come forward."

Daniel walked forward. He stepped onto the dais and faced Prospero.

"Lord Daniel," Prospero said, "will you accept the care of those who remain? To shepherd them as I have, these many years?"

Not that he had much choice. Say no, and they could tear him apart like a roast chicken.

"I will," he said.

"Then I give this back to you," Prospero said, holding out his sword cane with both hands. Daniel took it gravely. "And this," Prospero continued, "as a sign of your authority." He lifted the red ribbon and badge from his neck and slipped it over Daniel's head. It matched the lining of his coat.

Prospero faced the crowd. "I present to you: Lord Daniel!"

"Lord Daniel!" cried the Blessed.

"Now go," Prospero said. "Go to the bridges. Be ready to run." He smiled this time, a full one. "And to feast on new lands."

Now they cheered. They *roared*, and pressed for the exit like a swarm of trapped bees.

Even the string quartet, carrying their instruments.

We were left alone, the three of us, and Crow, among the dying roses, the flickering flames, and the lonely, graceful statue.

"My Lord," I said. "You can't do this. You can't just—sacrifice yourself!"

"Now, now, child. Where is your respect for your Elder? Accompany me one last time. One last adventure, Jessica. You would not deny me that, would you?"

"Of course not, my Lord." All the while I was thinking furiously of how to stop... whatever it was. Tackle him? I didn't trust my own fighting skills enough, and I definitely didn't want Daniel in the fray. And if I attacked him here, I stood no chance of knowing what he was trying to do, what magic he had harnessed to free the Blessed.

"Lord Daniel," he said, clapping Daniel on the shoulder. "Are you prepared?"

"This *is* something of a surprise—" Daniel admitted.

Prospero waved away the words. "You will do well. I know, because your strength has already proven itself. Come, children," he said, stepping lightly down. "We go."

I snuck a look at Crow, hoping Aunt Belinda had caught all this. "Where are we going, my Lord?"

"To Central Park," he said, merrily. And with a swirl of his cape, he strode down the aisle.

Daniel and I had time for one look at each other before we both jogged after him. The sanctuary doors opened to the dark stairs that led to the entryway. Prospero was out the front door, Daniel on his heels, when I heard a thump behind me in the dark foyer, and a swoosh of air, as if a giant moth had fallen off the ceiling. I turned, my train whipping around.

My eyes had barely adjusted, but I could see the flash of a crown in the darkness. And the white glow of a coat, edged with black, that Lily had sewn. A moth indeed.

Berron.

"What are you doing here?" I said. "I thought everyone was staying outside."

"You thought I'd miss a *royal* ball?"

"But—" I looked over my shoulder, sure that Prospero would be back through the door at any moment, catching "Jessica" chatting with the Prince of the Gentry.

"Get going, my Zelda," Berron said. "I'll be"—his fingers grazed my cheek—"right behind you."

Good God. This man. Prince. Fae. Gentry. Whatever! I gathered my train, shot him one last look, and ran for the red door.

The night was escaping.

And so were the Blessed.

29

Outside, the rest of the Blessed were long gone, presumably scattering to the bridges, ready to run across and start new lives of havoc in the outlying boroughs and beyond. Prospero and Daniel were walking in the direction of Central Park.

I put my legs to work. Crow soared alongside, visible only to me. When I caught up, I wasn't even breathing hard. Thank the Blessed for borrowed strength.

Prospero strolled without seeming to have a care in the world. His gaze traveled fondly over the Upper East Side buildings. "You would not think," he said, "having been trapped here so long, that I would miss this place."

"My Lord, what exactly is happening?" I asked. "Why are you not coming back?"

"Never before have you had so many questions, Jessica," Prospero said. "Have patience. All will be revealed."

Then, a voice buzzed in my ear: *Zelda, this is Aunt Belinda. If you can hear me, touch your crown.*

I touched it.

Good. I heard everything so far. Everyone's closing in. You want 'em to jump that guy?

Having Prospero jumped sounded appealing. But if I stopped him now, I'd never know his plans. Never know if there was a connection to the Forest of Emeralds. Never find a key to undo whatever had been done—and it was possible I'd never have a better chance.

I had to keep going.

I gave my head a tiny shake.

Okay, girl, Aunt Belinda responded in my ear. *Your call. You be careful. Your mama'd kill me if anything happened to you.*

I almost smiled. With family, you spend at least half of your time reminding each other to be careful.

We were almost at Fifth Avenue, the eastern border of Central Park. We stood at the crosswalk, waiting for the light to change, Upper East Siders streaming past in either direction studiously pretending there was nothing weird about three people dressed in full costumes in the middle of summer.

Déjà vu. I'd done this all before: the Upper East Side, a royal costume, a party. That one ended in flashing knives and vampire bargains.

The stoplight changed, and the white pedestrian symbol lit up. Magic everywhere, and still we obeyed technology.

Now—into Central Park.

Prospero gestured toward a sign. "To the North Woods."

To the North Woods, where a field of star fruit-scented flowers waited for sunrise.

Where the Arcade waited in her ice field.

The Arcade.

I'd been right all along. There *was* a connection. Prospero had made some kind of deal—a deal he didn't expect to walk away from—in exchange for releasing the Blessed into the wider world.

The paved sidewalks gave way to footpaths through ferns. With Prospero ahead of us, Daniel and I shared another uneasy glance.

Prospero began to whistle.

The forest opened up to the small clearing I had visited once before with Victorine. We approached the white flowers, which glowed innocently like starlight.

"One last adventure, my friends. One last adventure. Shall we?" Prospero said. His fangs showed: white ivory, sharp as fileting knives. He nicked his finger, and let a drop of blood fall. It spattered the white flowers with dark dots. The ground rumbled, he stepped forward, and he was gone.

I turned to Daniel. I'd been unable to speak this whole time, and now the words were bursting to come out. "This is your chance. Get out of here. If the spell falls, you can at least escape Manhattan."

"And let you go in there alone? What do you think I am?" His fangs elongated. He held my gaze as he slid the tip of his little finger against a point. "Manhattan is home." Blood welled, but he held his finger so it wouldn't fall. Waiting for me.

I hesitated. I wanted him to come. I wanted him to run.

Not so very different from our entire relationship, really.

But the moment was interrupted by a familiar voice behind us. "Ugh, so messy," Berron said. He stepped out of the woods, spotless despite traveling through the North Woods just like we had.

"Get out of here, man," Daniel said. "He'll know the jig is up if you come through with us."

Berron smirked. "Poor, simple Danny. Not if you put a sword to my heart when I get there."

"Just let him come, it's faster than arguing," I said.

Daniel frowned. "Fine." He paused, pointed a finger at Berron. "And it's 'Lord Daniel' to you."

Great time for a joke. I almost laughed.

Then Daniel and I held our hands over the white flowers, and at last, the blood fell. We took the small step into the flowers together, leaving Berron behind, but knowing he was—as he said at the church—right behind me.

The ground shook, and changed places with the sky.

I landed harder than when I'd dived onto that table to save Patty Melt from Aloysius the crazy owl. As dark as the summer night had been, it was darker now. And cold—*so* cold. Adrenaline and my real clothing were the only things holding in warmth. The ghostly costume was still in place.

I lifted my head, saw Daniel beside me, looking winded but whole. Still with it enough to be wary. Around us, the snowy field littered with boulders, the unfamiliar stars overhead a reminder that this was no ordinary place. Ahead, Prospero's cape thrashed in the icy wind. He barely seemed to notice, his head back and his arms open as if welcoming it.

Daniel and I got to our feet, brushing away snow. We flanked Prospero.

Prospero's hair glittered where ice had already crystallized. He lowered his arms. "It is time." His eyes glowed redder than usual. I wanted to call it evil, to keep it in the realm of something I could hate, but it wasn't. It was the fervor of doing what he believed, with all his heart—bag of dust or not—to be right.

"Not so fast." Berron's voice rang out.

Prospero, Daniel, and I turned, a united front of vampires, or so it seemed.

Of course, if Berron were really trying to be sneaky, he wouldn't have issued a verbal warning. He would have simply impaled Prospero on one of those sharp sticks without a word. But Berron was playing the same game I was: not to kill Prospero, but to find out what magic had been done to tangle the dimensions and sicken the Forest of Emeralds.

Daniel drew the sword from the cane, and rushed Berron.

It took half a second to realize that I—Jessica—should be doing the same thing. I ran at Berron, too, hoping no one got too sword- or stake-happy and turned me into a kebab.

Berron threw me off with far too much enjoyment, but let Daniel take him down, putting on a good show of struggling mightily until Daniel pressed the tip of the blade under Berron's rib cage, where it threatened to slide all the way to his heart.

Prospero approached, and gazed down upon Berron. "Prince of the Fae," he said. "You, of all beings, understand. You would do anything for your people, as I have done for mine. It is only that what you want, and what I want, cannot coexist. Know this, in the moment of your defeat: it was well-fought. But you have lost all the same." He pivoted away, toward the opposite horizon, as if catching a scent on the frigid air, Berron entirely forgotten. "Do you hear them?" he said. "The bells!"

Laughter made musical. So sweet. So light. So pretty.

Pretty doesn't always mean *good*.

Swirls of light danced across the landscape, an aurora borealis of magic, more powerful than an elemental witch, or the Blessed, or the Gentry. Pure, uncut power. The kind of power that could create artifacts from nothing, bend dimensions, fulfill wishes like an arctic genie. I didn't know, when I accepted one of the Arcade's gifts, that the price was so high.

I knew better now.

"I am ready, Arcade," Prospero called into the rising wind. "I have done as you asked. I have given you the power you require. The realm of the Gentry fades away even now. Take what I have given you. Use it. Break the spell."

The light coalesced, and the Arcade appeared, sparkling crystal ice in a female form, draped in icy robes that covered her hands, great lengths of glassy hair that drifted, weightless, through the cold air. Beautiful. Inhuman. So bright it was hard to look at her directly.

Her blowtorch eyes fixed on me.

I flinched. I knew, in an instant, that she saw through me. She had given me the mask, after all. My costume was no better than a child's plastic Superman cape.

She would reveal me to Prospero. We would never find out what had happened. All would be lost. Yet as this terrible reality loomed—unbelievably—her gaze shifted away.

To Prospero.

She wasn't going to reveal me. And it couldn't be because she didn't *know*. She knew. But she wouldn't risk revealing me, for fear of him changing his mind. Whatever it was, she wanted it *that much*.

She hovered closer, her glowing gaze still on Prospero. *You give yourself up willingly?*

"I am willing."

To become my host, that I may escape this dead world?

"Take me and walk free. I ask only that you free my people in return."

To take him and walk free! So that was the bargain, the unholy bargain he'd made to release the Blessed from their island prison: to be taken over by a creature of magic, and unleash her into a world entirely unprepared for a goddess to walk down Broadway. The magic of the Forest of Emeralds? Berron's sister, and the rest of the Gentry? Gone, fuel for the Arcade's escape.

And what would become of my new home when the Arcade was unleashed?

This couldn't happen. I had to stop it. Yet as powerful as I felt in my world, here, versus the Arcade, I felt powerless. Fire wouldn't harm the Arcade. No wind I could conjure would blow as strong as hers. Berron's magic with plants wouldn't work in this wasteland, and I didn't much rate Daniel's speed and strength against a being who swallowed magic from entire dimensions.

The Arcade's drifting hair curled and uncurled like octopus tentacles. *Long and long have I been imprisoned, yet I heed the old ways. Say it a second time, Lord Prospero, that your intentions be without a doubt.*

"I am willing."

Her eyes narrowed as she floated directly in front of Prospero. One of her long tresses curled around his neck. *Thrice is the charm. Say it once more.*

Prospero hesitated.

Time slowed.

Time stopped.

And then, from another dimension altogether—from the dimension of memory, nudged forward by a little fire mouse rummaging in the files—

My grandmother's voice.

From the carefree days I played in Central Park. From when we stood over a cutting board and I learned the right way to wield a knife. From when she taught me to be like her. To be the conduit to others' magic.

Strong and sure: *Let the magic in.*

I saw the Arcade before me, a being of crackling energy, a live wire. *It's too much*, I thought. *I'll die.*

Prospero stood before the Arcade, one sentence away from being obliterated, an old-fashioned gentleman facing the firing squad. Facing his own sacrifice and saying, *Yes.* The same Prospero that stepped around a dying Daniel in his Gramercy Park apartment. *Great generals are rarely understood by the rank and file*, he'd said.

I finally understood Prospero. I didn't have to like him, but I *understood.* Giving himself up completely.

He loved the Blessed.

And when it comes to love, there's really no choice at all.

I loved, too. Daniel. Berron. Berron's sister, trapped under the apple tree. Poppy and Lily and Aunt Belinda; Victorine; even Jessica, who didn't deserve to have an ancient fury unleashed.

But mostly—

Jester. Because I couldn't look him in his sweet, dumb face and tell him Mama hadn't tried to save the world.

Maybe it wouldn't work. Maybe I didn't have a chance.

Hell with it.

I was going to *try*.

"I am willing," Prospero said, for the third and final time.

The bells that rose were shriller than laughter, more piercing than a siren. They would have shattered glass. White light poured from the Arcade's eyes, from her mouth, and wrapped Prospero in glowing ropes. Her embrace enveloped the two of them and shined until the brightness made me close my eyes. Still the fire burned on my eyelids.

They were lost in their own spell, and I had no time to lose.

I turned away, to Daniel and Berron, who had already given up the pretense of fighting, Daniel helping Berron to his feet. "You have to help me hold on," I said.

"To what?" Daniel said.

I jerked my head at the blinding light. "To the Arcade."

"Zelda, no!" Berron lunged at me.

He missed. I was already gone. My speed was Victorine's, Daniel's, and Jessica's. I ran at the Arcade and threw my arms around her glowing form.

There was just enough time to smell a fine cologne, and the scent of meadows and rain; feel their arms around me, bracing me, crushing the corsage against my shoulder—and I smiled, knowing at least I wasn't alone, when the world blew apart.

Magic had always crept onto me, before. Thorny vines from the Blessed. Silver flames from Poppy, icy lace from my brother or Aunt Belinda. Green and gold vines from Berron. Prickly or smooth, hot or cold, they were—manageable.

This.

This was something else.

Electricity from the spinning planets. Songs in the key of the bones of the earth. Lightning splitting pine trees. All of it blazing through me until I thought it would stop my heart.

Still I held on.

More, I thought. *Is that all you got?*

And for the first time in my life, I didn't just wait for the magic. I grabbed and pulled with everything I had. I was as tall as the clouds. As tall as the sky. Looking down with eyes that saw into other worlds: the Shadows; the Forest of Emeralds; this blasted ice field—

And home.

I squeezed the Arcade tighter, feeling my arms become the arms of galaxies, my skin dotted with stars brushed from Jester's coat, sparkles of luck that never went away.

More.

What I held in my embrace changed. It wasn't the Arcade anymore.

It was draped in old-fashioned velvet and shaped like a man. Prospero—but not Prospero.

Prospero was gone.

The Arcade had taken him over completely.

My arms were galaxies, and I held him—the shell of him—and wept tears for Prospero from the cracked moons of my eyes.

More.

Magic overflowed. I was magic itself, shedding stardust waterfalls onto the Forest of Emeralds, so much that it ran off the side like water spilling off a dinner plate. Doors flew open and eternity spun through me, the stars going out, one by one, candles in an abandoned church, finally exhausted.

The last sparks pulled Daniel, Berron, and I out—home—slamming the door on the Arcade, and Prospero, forever, with a blast of smoke like star fruit on fire.

Something, somewhere, shattered with a sound like falling chandeliers.

Before everything went black, I might have seen God.

And he may have been a little black poodle.

30

I f you have to wake up sandwiched between two someones, they should at least smell good. It takes the edge off the urge to scream.

It does not, however, make up for drool on your pillow, sweat soaking your clothes, and rats' nests in your hair. Especially when you have no idea where you are, how you got there, and why there is a nice-smelling man on either side of you.

Pillows. Pillows everywhere. This is familiar, somehow. So is the sound.

A horse. Yes, it's definitely a horse, neighing. And where is that apple scent coming from?

I sat up. Big mistake. Someone hammered a saute pan on my head, or at least it felt like it, and my mouth tasted like grill scrapings. The room was dim, the only light coming from a couple of golden sconces. And we were in a sumptuous heap of bedding strewn with bits of dried flowers and herbs.

Ah.

Berron's bed.

I looked to my right.

Berron, sound asleep. Or passed out.

To my left, Daniel. Same.

"Huh," I said, scratching my head in an attempt to remember exactly what happened last night. On closer inspection, Berron had a nasty cut on his forehead. I brushed Berron's hair aside for a better look.

"Right behind you," he muttered, before rolling over sleepily and nestling back into the pillows.

I blinked at him. Hadn't I heard that before? Recently?

I shifted to face Daniel, and patted his shoulder. "Daniel, wake up."

"Lord Daniel," he murmured.

"Lord Daniel, my ass," I said.

But he, too, rolled over and continued sleeping.

"Bunch of help you two are." But something about the words, even as they left my mouth, gave me pause. As if I knew on some level they weren't accurate at all. What *had* happened last night? Why were we in Berron's room in the Fortress of Apples?

I threw off the coverlet and looked down at myself. Saw I wasn't disguised in the Empress costume anymore. Crown and comb missing in action. I'd reverted to my real appearance: middle-aged Zelda, Peaseblossom outfit, minus my Doc Martens.

I wiggled my toes.

Had someone taken my shoes off? Had I? My fuzzy brain reached for the chain of events between point A, at Poppy's house, and point B, in Berron's bed.

Surely there was a really good explanation somewhere. One that didn't require moving back to Florida to escape the shame.

The horse neighed again.

Sybelia!

And then, a voice. Mellow and smooth, a female voice, like a wind instrument in a lower register. I didn't know anyone who sounded like that. And even if I did, they wouldn't be here, in a dying, silent world. I pushed myself up and off the bed, my feet bumping into where my shoes had been placed neatly at the foot, next to a sparkly crown and a hair comb—and a corsage that looked like it'd been ironed. I tugged on my boots. "Hey," I called, heading for the door. "Who's there?" With that, I pushed the stone door open and stepped through.

And froze.

The apple orchard had burst to life. Every green leaf glowed, every apple blushed more ripe than rubies. The great trees of the Forest of Emeralds rose in the distance, supporting a sky turned from sickly dark green to clear aquamarine blue. Clouds like horses' tails. A scent like nothing I'd ever smelled before: fresh grass and healthy dirt and green sap and water rich with minerals, the kind of scent I could fall asleep to and wake up to and have a smile on my face the whole time.

But even that was nothing compared to what I saw beneath the trees.

People.

Not just any people.

The Gentry.

Awake, free, *alive*. Running beneath the trees, dancing with colorful ribbons, laughing and falling down and getting up again. Juggling apples. Playing catch. Embracing. Young, middle-aged, and old, dressed in all the colors of the rainbow and possibly a few more.

Soft thuds on the turf announced Sybelia's approach. On her back, a young lady dressed all in gold, crowned with gold, wielding a handful of golden magic to sprinkle stars through the air like confetti. They stopped a few feet away, and the golden child—Berron's sister—slid down from Sybelia's back, revealing a carved wooden bow slung against her back. "Zelda," she said, and of course the beautiful voice was hers.

I swallowed. Despite being younger and smaller than Berron, she was twice as intimidating. "Hi," I said.

Possibly not my best moment.

She held out both hands, and her sweet smile was both enchanting and genuine. "I am the Princess of Arrows."

"Princess of Arrows," I repeated. I was so dazzled I almost forgot to take her extended hands.

Her warm fingers held mine. "You saved us."

I shook my head. "No—"

"Be not bashful, O Zelda."

Bashful? Far from it. Amnesiac, more like. I was having trouble forming words, though. Her Gentry magic was already climbing my wrists, wrapping them in molten gold.

"Do you not remember? My brother and his companion, the Lord Daniel, carried you hence."

"They *carried* me?"

"Yes—after the Prince's wound was tended. According to the Lord Daniel, my brother struck his head on a boulder when they were thrown from holding you."

Good *God*, what had happened?

"The Lord Daniel stopped the bleeding with his jacket."

Cobweb, I thought instantly. *Cobwebs staunch blood*, Lily said. Goosebumps lit up my arms. And why was Berron's sister calling him Lord Daniel—

Then I remembered.

The cane changing hands. The medal on the blood-red ribbon. The walk from the church to Central Park, with Prospero. Into the field of starfruit-smelling flowers, into the ice field strewn with boulders. Prospero giving himself up to the Arcade. Throwing myself at the two of them. Expanding to the size of the universe, all that power nearly blowing me apart as Berron and Daniel helped me hang on.

My eyes closed and the ground tilted.

Her grip shifted, and I felt her arm go around my waist. "You should lie down, dear friend."

I liked that. *Dear friend*. Like *my Zelda*, but less claim. Too bad the Forest of Emeralds was sliding out from under me, or I could have thought about it some more. "No," I said. "Not in there. I'll just sit on the grass."

She helped me sink to the green, as soft as any bed. I meant to sit, but somehow I kept going until I was lying on my back, gazing up at the sky and the horsetail clouds.

Everything was perfect. Everything was beautiful.

"You know who would like this place a lot?" I said.

The Princess of Arrows kneeled beside me. "Who?"

"My dog." Now that I'd thought of him, I couldn't stop thinking of him. Did he sleep well without me? Did he get his usual treats, snacks, and walks?

A stone door clicked open behind my head, and two figures emerged.

"Lying down on the job?" Daniel said.

They came around in front of me. From the ground, they looked like giants. Giants messy from sleep, but still. Cobweb and Moth.

And me, Peaseblossom.

A powerful love potion, Lily had said. Not hearts and flowers and candy. This love meant being afraid—and doing the thing anyway, because there's nothing more important than protecting what you love.

That was the kind of love potion I was.

The spinning settled into a gentle rocking that would have been kind of nice, if I didn't have things to do. I sat up and held my hands out to Berron and Daniel.

They pulled me up, and the three of us embraced. "Thank you," I said.

Normally, Berron would have had a clever comeback. Instead, he kissed my cheek lightly.

"Sorry about your head," I added.

"Be sorry for me," Daniel said, adding a kiss on my other cheek, not to be outdone. "He ruined my jacket. With his *blood*." He made a face.

I laughed.

"Well," Berron said, his eyes dancing, "he kept trying to make me call him 'Lord' Daniel."

"That's because I *am* Lord Daniel."

I stared at him. "You didn't mean that—" I looked around. The Princess of Arrows had slipped away with Sybelia. "You were just playing along."

Daniel looked away. "I may have made a tiny deal with the Arcade."

I punched his arm. "You bastard. You told everyone you'd fallen straight through. I *trusted* you." Daniel tried to take my arm. I shrugged him off. "What deal did you make?"

"I did it for the right reasons—"

"*What deal did you make?*"

"To replace Prospero."

My mouth fell open.

"He was a bad dude, all right? Maybe the Blessed and the Gentry can stop killing each other, you know, if someone new is in charge."

"You," I said.

He shrugged.

Berron looked like he was barely containing his glee. Not because Daniel was in charge. Because Daniel was in trouble.

With me.

I sighed. Rubbed my temples. Wished it had all stayed simple: a normal ex-boyfriend, and a Brooklyn hipster with remarkable wood-working abilities. And now here I was with the Lord of the Blessed and the Prince of the Gentry.

I held my finger up, a caution and a threat. Pointed first at Daniel, then Berron, who widened his eyes innocently. I swung the finger back to Daniel, poked him in the chest. "Got anything else you want to share with the class?"

"That's it," he said, holding his hands up.

It made a kind of sense, what he said about the Blessed and the Gentry. Not that I'd ever tell *him* that. He didn't deserve the satisfaction.

He could sweat.

I turned back to Berron, who took a step back. "And you. Getting drunk and proposing to make me the Queen of the Gentry. Calling me 'my Zelda.'"

"Not your Zelda," Daniel murmured.

"Shut up," I said. I looked Berron in the eyes, but it was hard, because rather than looking abashed, he looked like he was remembering something delicious. My cheeks flamed as the memory of the kiss in the Flatiron Saloon came back unbidden.

I pressed on. "You have to"—I paused, searched for the right words—"you have to dial it back."

"Dial it back?" Berron said.

"Yes," I said, with a sureness I didn't feel. "I mean, your sister called me 'dear,' and that didn't bother me."

A huge silence.

"So, you want me to act like my sister."

"Yes."

"Mm-hm," he said, lingering over it. Disbelieving. Giving me a look that would drop angels in their tracks. "No problem, dear Zelda."

I took a deep breath. "Now let's go home. I have a boy to kiss."

They exchanged glances.

"One who's covered in fur. Lead the way to the Mirror."

"About that," Daniel said.

"Oh, no," I said, the sound of shattering crystal coming back with terrifying clarity. "Aunt Belinda will be worried sick. And Poppy! And Jester—"

"It's okay," Berron said. "After we made sure you were safe, we went out and let them know what happened. That's why we both slept in."

"But how did you get out if the Mirror was gone?"

Berron smiled. "You opened all the old ways."

"*I* opened the old ways?"

He nodded.

"*All* of them?"

"Every single one. In fact," he said, "I think you have a few visitors coming through now."

A black shape flew down the path between the apple trees, paws extended like a tiny race horse, barely touching the ground, mouth open, ears a-flapping, tongue waving joyfully like a skinny pink flag.

"Jester!" I cried, sinking to the grass in time to catch him like a furry cannonball. He was everywhere, paws and claws and kisses and tail pouf wagging, making snuffly noises as if he just couldn't sniff me enough. "It's been a *million years*, I know, boy." I hugged him, ran my hand over his silky, fluffy ears. He licked my face, the little opportunist.

Hoofbeats on the turf announced the return of Sybelia. This time, it wasn't the Princess of Arrows on her back.

It was Poppy—and Georgiana running alongside, shaggy hair swishing with each great bound. Poppy brought Sybelia to a neat stop as Georgiana ran circles around our little group, Jester bouncing away to join in the frolic. Poppy tossed her leg over Sybelia's back and slid down, landing on the grass as gracefully as a magic trick. "Ta-da!" she said, opening her arms.

I threw my arms around her. "Mustardseed!"

"Peaseblossom, you scamp. Running off to the Arcade without so much as a how-do-you-do. Haven't I told you not to do that? Very naughty."

I hugged her harder. "I'm sorry."

We both laughed, breaking apart, as the dogs collided with us in search of more scritchy-scratchies and kisses.

"Have they told you?" Poppy said.

"Told me what? That the old ways are open?"

"That's not all," she said. "Come on."

We left the Fortress of Apples behind and entered the Forest, walking into the deep woods, far from where we had gone before. Jester and Georgiana stopped to sniff at every exposed tree root and forest flower. What had seemed so dark and forbidding before had changed completely. The moss almost bounced under my feet. The tree trunks were so richly colored they looked carved from chocolate, like Christmas log cakes stood on end, soaring upward to green umbrella canopies, the blue sky peeking through with clean, pure light.

We reached a cove where two trees bent toward each other, their branches so deeply entwined, they'd begun to merge.

The Princess of Arrows stood to the side of the arch, her golden gown shifting slightly in a sweet breeze. Waiting.

Daniel pulled out leashes from his pocket and snapped them on Jester and Georgiana, standing by. Ready.

Berron bowed to his sister. "Princess of Arrows. Our guests will return home." He paused, catching my gaze. "For now."

The Princess regarded us. "Fare you well, travelers. It is my fondest wish that you return to the Forest of Emeralds soon, to celebrate in the proper fashion."

"Yes, Your Highness," Poppy said, with one of those full-size curtsies.

Berron held out his hand to me. "Ready?"

"Where does this go?" I said.

"You'll see."

I hung back for only a second. When you've walked through mirrors, fallen through dimensions, and battled a goddess of magic, what's one little archway? I took Berron's hand, and Poppy's. Poppy took Daniel's. Daniel's free hand had both leashes, Jester and Georgiana happily tangling themselves in knots.

We went through.

Unlike the Mirror, which seemed to billow cold air when crossed, this archway breathed the same scent as the Forest of Emeralds, enveloping us in comfortable coolness before fading away. Suddenly we were knee-deep in bushes, neck-deep in vines, and surrounded by summer heat.

"Where are we?" I said, pushing at the foliage where it seemed thinnest. The tangle gave way with a sudden release, and I found myself standing on a neatly raked gravel path bordered by rounded shrubbery and deep green park benches. Ahead, a bronze statue of a man rose, surrounded by flowers. Beyond that, a fence of evenly spaced black metal bars topped with decorative gold points.

This was Gramercy Park. We were inside the locked, private, Gramercy Park.

Before, the garden had stopped at the fence.

Now it overflowed the street and climbed up the surrounding buildings.

They looked, at first, like green walls. Living green walls, many stories high, dotted with flowers, alive with more butterflies than I'd ever seen in one place. Stone blocks and Gothic windows peeked through gaps in the foliage, as if green blankets had been haphazardly thrown over the buildings. New bushes had sprung up like mushrooms in the park itself, bearing even more flowers. Trees stretched higher and greener as if life had poured into their roots in a great rush, causing them to stretch toward the sky. New vines wrapped the fences and spilled onto the sidewalk.

A real urban jungle. The Forest of Emeralds had taken over this bit of Manhattan.

Berron, Poppy, and Daniel joined me on the gravel path.

"What did I do?" I said.

"Redecorated," Berron said. "It's like this everywhere."

"Everywhere? What do you mean, 'everywhere'?"

"Every green space. Everywhere there's a connection. Daniel and I saw it while you were resting."

I thought of Central Park. Riverside Park. Dozens more. All connected, all blooming. From a stardust waterfall of pure magic. What would the elemental witches think of this very public explosion of magic? What would the Blessed do, after the spell didn't fall, and the city parks overflowed with green? "I didn't know this was going to happen," I said, taking Jester's leash from Daniel.

Poppy took Georgiana's leash. "Well done," she said. "Adding a little excitement to the day."

"Understatement of the century," Daniel said, straightening his collar. "Ready to go home?"

"How?" I said, unable to tear my gaze away from the greenery. "It's locked."

"I can fix that," Daniel said, lifting the medal that hung around his neck. It turned out to not be a medal at all, but a large locket, which opened like a pocket watch, and held a gold-toned key, modern and sturdy, stamped with a number. Daniel snapped the medal shut and flourished the key. "Found it this morning. Goes with the apartment," he said, nodding in the direction of Prospero's building.

Daniel's building.

The golden key slid into the lock. Daniel pulled the handle and held the gate open.

A giant purple butterfly that didn't look quite real flapped past us. Jester pulled so hard after it his little paws scrabbled on the path. Was it from our world, or not? And where would it lead, if I followed it?

A summer breeze carried a hint of burned star fruit, and I thought of the first time I met the Arcade: *You will go where you have never been. And you will become what you never were.*

She was right—I *had* gone where I had never been—but she was wrong. I didn't become what I never was.

I became who I was always meant to be: someone who loved my dog, my friends, and my family, balancing spells and sandwiches in a city of steel, stone, and magic, following a poodle and a purple butterfly to my next adventure.

Those chiming bells in the distance?

Probably nothing but an ice cream truck.

⸺❧⸺

ALSO BY KATE MOSEMAN

Spells and Sandwiches
Flames and Frying Pans
Witch and Wolfhound

Silver Spells
Silver Charms
Silver Dreams
Silver Shadows

A Good Demon Is Hard to Find
A Witch's Work Is Never Done
An Angel in My Teacup

Roller Coaster Romance

www.ingramcontent.com/pod-product-compliance
Lightning Source LLC
Chambersburg PA
CBHW020747190726
48285CB00006B/1919